# CHAINED TO THE CHAMPION

## DRAKARN MATES
### BOOK 5

KATE RUDOLPH

**One broken warrior. One defiant spy. A deadly mission with one rule: trust each other or die.**

Captured and stranded near the hostile city of Ignarath, Drakarn warrior Zarvash and human intelligence officer Vega Cross must rely on each other to survive. Their mission? Infiltrate the enemy city where humans are enslaved and warriors fight in savage arena battles. Their cover? Master and slave.

The roles are fake. The bond awakening between them is all too real.

As they fight side by side—Zarvash in the blood-soaked tournament, Vega in the shadows of a brutal alien city—their connection deepens into something fierce and undeniable. But when their secret is uncovered, and Vega faces death in the arena,

Zarvash must risk everything to claim the woman who's become his fated mate.

**Fans of possessive alien heroes, kick-butt heroines, and fated mates romance will devour this action-packed sci-fi love story.**

## ZARVASH

The darkness was absolute.

It was an oppressive, weight-crushing vision, heavier than any sleep. This void was an insult; a cage built of stolen light. Then, there was agony. It lanced through my skull, starting where my scales scraped against something cold.

I fought the blackness, tried to command limbs that refused to answer. I was bound. The tight, coarse material bit deep, grinding against hide, against bone. Humiliation burned hotter than the pain. My wings were in agony. They were wrenched back, twisted grotesquely, joints screaming a silent protest. Fury clawed at my throat.

Grounded, flightless. A warrior stripped of his sky is less than nothing.

Blood filled my mouth, sharp and metallic. My stomach tightened with anger. I carefully worked my jaw, ignoring the fresh pulse of agony through my skull. I was unbroken. It was a small mercy in this degradation.

"... waste of resources ..." The voice grated, harsh and thick with the unmistakable, sloppy cadence of the Ignarath. It was like stones scraping stone. Contemptible.

"Orders are orders." The second voice was smoother yet carried the same underlying arrogance. "They pay well for live ones."

Live ones. Tactical awareness cut through the pain. I made myself stay still and listen. It was the only defense I had left. Stillness was a shield; information, a blade waiting to be drawn. They needed to think I was broken.

"The female's useless," the first grunted, closer now. The scrape of his talons on unseen stone set my teeth on edge. "Human. She won't survive."

Human? The word struck like a physical blow. Female. Images fractured behind the darkness—the scouting mission, the sudden chaos, Ignarath filth pouring from the rocks. Was it Kira? No ... Terra? Darrokar's mate? Impossible. He would have leveled this mountain range. Who else? Khorlar would have died fighting.

Who?

A guttural snort followed. "It's double price for humans now."

Then, something else cut through the stench of blood and the cold dampness of the stone. A scent bloomed in the stale air, impossibly sweet, complex. It was like fire-nectar blooms, yes, but laced with something ... alien. Utterly foreign, yet it resonated deep within my bones, a vibration beneath the pain. My nostrils flared, drawing it in against my will. It invaded my senses like fine smoke, bypassing thought, settling somewhere primal. My fangs ached —a sharp, unfamiliar pang. The very air seemed to thicken, growing textured against my tongue.

"Check the bronze one's restraints," the calmer voice commanded, closer now. "He's dangerous."

Heavy talons scraped stone, approaching. Every instinct screamed to tear free, to rend and shatter, but I forced stillness. Weakness is a cloak.

"Still out," the first grunted. "I hit him hard enough." A sharp prod dug into my shoulder, finding a nasty wound I hadn't fully registered. Pain flared, white-hot. I clamped my jaw, biting back the instinctive growl, tasting blood anew.

Then the scent intensified. It was overwhelming. Closer. Something warm, impossibly soft, pressed against my side. Heat radiated through thin fabric, against my scales. Not stone. Not metal. Life. Small, rhythmic breaths, too fast for my kind. A human. Her. The realization struck like lightning, rearranging the landscape of my pain.

The scent poured from her, wrapping around my senses, drowning the stench of Ignarath and damp rock. It filled my head, overwhelming, drawing me toward her against all sense.

"He's waking up," a voice snarled from my other side. A vicious kick landed squarely on my ribs, stealing my breath. "Dose him again."

"Waste of venom. We'll be at the exchange by nightfall."

Movement beside me told me she stirred, the woman—the source of the scent. A soft sound, feminine, fragile, bypassed reason, striking a deep, resounding chord within my chest. It was possessive. Primal. My muscles bunched, straining futilely against the unyielding bindings.

"Separate them," the calmer one ordered sharply. "He's reacting. I've seen this filth before."

"Disgusting," spat the first. "Scalvaris heathens.

Mating with off-worlders." Another kick slammed into my wounded side, fueled by contempt.

She made another sound. It was pained. A soft whimper that ignited a bonfire of fury within me. A growl tore from my throat, low and vicious, shattering my facade of unconsciousness. I was exposed.

"See? Told you." Rough hands fumbled near my head, grabbing at the binding over my eyes, then pausing. "Leave him blind. It's less trouble."

"Move her."

"No ...," her voice came. Barely a whisper, yet it rang through my bones like a struck shield. A challenge. A claim?

Hands seized her, dragging the warmth, the scent, away. Illogical panic clawed through me. The sudden emptiness beside me was an agony sharper than any physical wound. The scent faded, pulling my focus, my strength, with it.

"Stop ..." The word was a broken rasp, torn from my throat. Darkness surged at the edges of the void, thicker now.

Pain pulsed, a relentless hammer against my skull, but beneath it, one imperative burned with the clarity of molten rock. This pull, this sudden, fierce certainty ... it wasn't confusion. It was recognition.

An awakening of something buried deep within the bedrock of my being.

Whoever she was, she belonged under my protection.

I had to find her. Shield her.

She was mine.

The blackness swallowed me whole once more.

PAIN WOKE ME—WORSE than any sunburn, worse than sore muscles. My wing throbbed, every movement—even each shallow breath—drove hot pokers deeper into bone. I filed it away. Pain was data. I mapped its limits with every exhale, assigned it numbers, classified it by urgency.

If I let it claim me, I would never get up again.

I forced my focus to the world. The suns beat overhead, heat crawling like ants beneath my scales. The air was raw-blood metallic, overlayed with something honey-sharp. The human. The scablands sprawled without mercy; wind ground sand in my teeth and shade melted before I could claim it. We were flanked by rock spires, boxed in but not unseen.

Our four Ignarath captors were sprawled between us and freedom: careless, sure of their dominance, claws idly raking dust. Golden brown scales caught sunlight, as if daring us to fight. My tactical brain ticked over. I tracked weapons—knives, teeth, the one with the short sword hanging carelessly. Distances: six steps to the nearest cover, two Ignarath within easy striking range, the farthest fiddling with a small blade.

Every detail was ammunition.

At my back, warmth pressed against me: human, alive, pulse snapping through the silence. Vega. I caught her scent—sweat and heat and something that made me stumble. Every beat of my heart demanded I shift my focus from the enemy to her. I bit the inside of my cheek as if that might help me regain control.

Now was the worst possible moment for this curse.

A shadow sliced across us. One Ignarath, Kerek, I'd heard the others call him, sauntered close, eyes gleaming predator yellow. He crouched, tongue flicking, gaze sliding over Vega's shape with greedy calculation. The urge to eviscerate him stoked fire under my scales. I counted heartbeats, forced my claws to stay hidden.

"Quiet, female." He jabbed her shoulder, grinning, too confidant. "Skorai will pay double. You'll keep him entertained."

I felt Vega's tension through our bound wrists, but it was rage, not fear. "I'm going to enjoy killing you," she spat, lacing it with contempt.

He barked a laugh, scattering dirt in her face, then swaggered away.

Amateur.

If they'd known they were holding Scalvaris's best tactician and a former human soldier, they might have used iron bindings. I flexed my tail; it was tied tight to my thigh, but the knot was rushed, unfinished. I mapped the rope's pattern blind with my scales, letting muscle memory work where pain tried to sabotage me.

Movement: six paces to my left, an Ignarath raising a canteen; count of three, the sentry would pass behind a pillar, vision blocked.

Vega's fingers tightened on mine, three quick pulses, pause, three more. Some kind of code. She noticed my subtle shift, or maybe just gambled; I respected both. She was asking for trust, dangerous, but we'd die chained together if I hesitated.

The rope gave. I worked my tail under her bindings next. Every twinge in my wing chiseled another threat of blackout behind my eyes. I squeezed back—go.

"Get them up. Move!" the command snapped. An Ignarath closed in, grabbing for Vega's arm.

No time left for strategy.

"Now," I hissed low.

She moved, a sharp headbutt to the Ignarath's mouth, bone crumpling with a wet crack. He shrieked, weapon hand flailing. Instinct vaulted us both into motion. I yanked my tail free, kicked upward, and twisted, positioning my body between the Ignarath and Vega. Pain convulsed through my wing, a paralyzing bolt, and I nearly buckled.

Not now.

I took shuddering inventory: three Ignarath left: one recovering, one drawing steel, one fumbling for his weapon. I swept low, feigning a drop, then snapped my claws across the closest one's calf, severing ligaments. He collapsed; I rolled, putting the broken body between me and the others, using every advantage.

Vega wasn't waiting. She moved with human unpredictability—duck, jab, elbow, stone to temple.

Messy, glorious.

A blade swung past my face. I barely saw it, senses blurring as something flared deep within me.

For half a second, scent and movement tangled, Vega's blood and heat dragging my feral instincts to the surface. I almost turned toward her, to shield rather than strike. I caught myself.

Focus!

The largest Ignarath charged. My left wing screamed as I tried to launch myself into the air, no flight, no leverage. I pivoted, jaws snapping, let his momentum carry him into my open claws. My fingers sank deep, blood washing over knuckles. My legs shook. Vega, to my right, smashed an Ignarath's knee, then drove a sharp rock into his gut; the man folded with a sob.

"Zarvash!" she barked a warning. One wounded captor staggered to his feet behind her, blade glimmering. Through haze and agony, I lunged, windpipe seizing as I forced my ruined wing to move, damn the cost. My claws locked on his arm. I twisted, feeling bone break beneath my grip, and buried fangs in his throat. Heat, thrashing, then limpness.

Vega had already finished her opponent, her arm streaked red to the elbow, eyes fever-wild, blood-red hair stuck to her brow in a tangled riot. Her gaze raked across me.

I wanted, against all reason, to drag her close, to scent her hair, to guard her as if she were mine.

I hated that I wanted it.

"Don't look at me like that." Her words cut sharp. She wiped her mouth with the back of her hand, grip still white-knuckled on her stone. "You look like you want to eat me."

The accusation snapped me awake. I stepped back. "If that were true, you'd be dead already."

She paced a wary circle, not turning her back to me. She eyed the Ignarath bodies, tensed like I might attack next, practical, not personal, which was almost worse. I wished I didn't deserve the distrust.

I crouched, rifling through the pockets of the dead for weapons; she mirrored the motion, taking her own loot, grabbing and testing a knife as insurance. The sun seared us. My wings ached, hot, useless weight. I tried to unfurl them.

Agony lanced up my spine, blind spots flickering my vision. They nearly cost me my life, twice now. I reminded myself to stop pretending they might miraculously heal in minutes.

"You fight like an amateur," I said, forcing my voice into something casual. "Messy, reckless."

She smirked, wiping blood from a split lip. "I'm alive. I'll take messy."

Complicated, this one. Not friend, not safe. I watched her shoulders, her hands on a looted flask, swigging the lifegiving water. Good. Smart. She tossed it my way, and I drained what I dared, reflex making me watch for a flinch or double-cross. None came.

For a moment, neither of us moved. The air sizzled between us, within me.

"So." Her tone was iron. "Where the hell are we?"

I scanned the horizon. Sand, stone, burnt desolation. Trackless, unfamiliar. They'd carried us for days in a rough sack, only setting us down in the dark until today. Heat-sheared rocks, unfamiliar glyphs scratched by claws I didn't recognize. We were nowhere near Scalvaris, that much was certain.

"I don't know."

Survival demanded discipline. I tore my attention to inventory: two water flasks, three knives, and one sidearm with two charges. Not enough for what was out there.

A shadow skittered on the ridge, something watching, waiting.

"We move east," I said, brusque, ignoring the ache in my wing, in my blood. "There's shade. Unless you want to wait for whatever that is." I nodded toward new tracks just visible in drifting sand: claws, wide-set, fresh.

She hesitated, but followed, knife steady in her fist, the closest thing to truce we had. Every step was cautious, uncertain, predatory.

Under Volcaryth's harsh suns, nothing was safe.

And something wild within me wanted the human beside me.

Hells.

CAMP, if you could even call it that, was a gouged patch of shadow under a spine of rock, the kind that looked like it wanted to collapse and finish the job the world had started on us. Bedding? Sure, if "wind-blown grit in every orifice" counted. My shoulders ached. My lips were split, and my tongue was dry like I'd been chewing sand for a year.

But none of that was the real problem.

The real problem was Zarvash.

He moved like a grenade with the pin out, hunched against the stone, pretending "intimidating" was a strategy instead of the last excuse holding his bones in place. His wing, torn, twisted at his side, had to hurt. He was trying to look stoic. He was pulling it off, too, in the way seven-foot murder-lizards always managed when pretending they didn't bleed.

Except he did. Bleed, I mean. Every time the wind hit him just right, I saw him flinch. It was tiny. Gone in a blink. But it was there, pulsing under the mountain of bronze scale like a warning sign only I bothered to read.

I sure as hell wasn't about to coddle a dragon, but letting him bleed out when I had no idea where we were? Even worse.

"Let me see the damage," I demanded. If I made it an order, maybe he'd listen. Or pretend to.

His head snapped around, eyes like twin gold razors in the firelight. "There's nothing to be done."

That was the wrong answer.

"Did I ask for your diagnosis, Doctor Deathwish? Show me your damn wing. Or do you want to limp home with half your insides on the outside?" Every syllable ground to an edge. No time for polite.

He stared. He was measuring me, probably trying to decide if I'd stab him or collapse first. But then, grudgingly, jaw clamped, he shifted. The bag he'd scavenged from our captors hit the ground. He eased out his wing with a care that probably cost him, even if he'd cut off his own tail before admitting it.

What he revealed was bad. Really bad. The membrane was a patchwork of torn flesh, blood congealed into sticky black ropes. The joint looked wrong, swollen, inflamed, fever bright. Then there were the gouges, deep enough that I could see the underlayer. Under all that scale and brute force, he was vulnerable.

"Shit." I leaned in. I couldn't help it. "How long has it been like this?"

"Since the battle." He bared his teeth. "There's no need to worry. I've lost more blood than this in training."

"Oh, wow. Do you want a trophy or just a pat on the nose? Stop posturing." I kept my voice low, but I wasn't doing gentle. Gentle was for safer worlds.

He'd been carrying this wound for days, ever since some assholes from Ignarath had managed to get the upper hand on both of us while we were fighting for our lives outside of Scalvaris. Judging by the fact that our captors hadn't met with any backup, I didn't think the fight went their way. But had anyone died? Hawk? That damned snarly mate of hers?

I had to push the worries out of my mind.

For now.

When I reached for his wing, I hesitated. Not

because I wanted to touch him, nope. But something about the heat radiating off him, power right there under my hands, made my skin tingle, anticipation spiking in every nerve. It didn't matter. I had a job to do. "Flex for me. Slow."

He did. There was a grinding noise you could feel in your molars, bone on bone. His tail lashed. Not at me. At the universe.

My hands hovered, steady but not steady enough. "It's not just torn. It looks infected."

He scoffed. "Drakarn wounds heal."

"Would Mysha agree with you?" I named the head healer of Scalvaris, and Zarvash flinched. I dug into my bag, cursed at the state of it. Our kidnappers hadn't been kind enough to furnish us with a first aid kit. "The least I can do is wash it out. Don't scream." I uncapped the water flask and poured it over his wound.

"I do not—" he started, but when I hit a tender tendon, he sucked in so hard you'd think the world shrank.

The air between us didn't just vibrate. It burned. It was just a bit of water, but it was like being stuck in a lightning storm under your skin, prickling, urgent, wrong. All the while, Zarvash just stared. He was unmoving, blank, but not blank enough: something wild there, coiled behind his eyes.

If he tried to eat me, I'd almost thank him for the distraction.

*God, girl, not now.*

I lingered too long. I knew it. I didn't move until every joint gleamed with moisture and my heartbeat had long since jumped to double time. Then I wiped my hands. "That's all you get. Try not to die before we get home."

He made a noise, low, a growl, maybe a laugh if you squinted. "Comforting. Your bedside manner would terrify even a lavabeast."

"Beats getting eaten by one." I didn't smile. I couldn't. "How far to Scalvaris? We've been walking for a while now; you must have a guess."

He retreated to the shadows, adjusted the useless wing like he could will it better. He kept his face hidden. At first, I figured he'd ignore me. A Drakarn trick I'd observed too many times: stretch the silence until your nerves snapped.

Then he spoke. "We are far beyond the Great Lava Lake. With my wing as it is, I can't fly us back. On foot, it's more than a moon's journey."

A cold pit opened in my gut. "That's ... You're not saying a month, are you?"

His gaze flickered. "Longer. With my wounds, longer still."

Great. A month with *him*. Why not just sign up for a six-course banquet, "me" as the main dish.

He kept talking like it cost him something, "Unless ..."

My head snapped up, reflex sharp as a blade. "Unless what? Unless I sprout wings?"

He didn't flinch. "Unless we make for Ignarath instead. It is near. Two days, maybe less. But—" He bared his teeth. "It is enemy ground for us both."

I wanted to laugh. Or maybe scream. "You're suggesting we walk right into the den of vipers that was trying to buy us?"

My original plan had been to make my way to Ignarath ... somehow. It was clear now just how foolish I'd been.

He gave a slow, rolling shrug. It was all muscle and implication. "It is a place. Plaktish made it clear they have humans, perhaps *your* humans. Bargaining chips. If we learn why, if we learn what Ignarath plans ... Scalvaris gains advantage. The Blade Council—"

I sliced through that with a glare sharp as glass. "You care about the council, fine. Since when do you give a shit about what happens to us? You don't even like humans." I hadn't forgotten what his scheming had almost cost Orla. I still wasn't sure why Rath hadn't ended this guy.

Zarvash's jaw flexed, and his scales rippled. "I do not." His words were blunt as a hammer. "But Ignarath grows bold. They are planning something. For what purpose, I do not know. If they seek war, I must know."

That. That right there, danger beating in the cracks, not hatred or loyalty, just rage at something bigger than either of us. I could almost taste that Ignararth envoy, Plaktish's oily voice, echoing between my ears. I remembered Khorlar, stone and fury, putting himself between me and the threat. I remembered the way every Drakarn got cagey when Ignarath came up. Even here, with Zarvash, the tension spread on my skin like poison.

"So, we sneak into a city run by killers and slavers, poke around, and hope we don't end up bartered for claws or chained in a basement? And that's your best plan?" I shot back, my words dry as desert bones.

His mouth twitched in something almost like a smile. "Alone, I can manage the terrain. With you—" He paused, the silence a knife between us. "You are ... slippery. That makes you useful."

Never just a person. Always a tool. My hand closed in a fist at my side, my nails digging grit. "So, this is just strategy. You trade me if things go bad?"

His eyes glittered with cold intelligence, nothing else. "Trading you gains me little. Ignarath wants it all. I want information. That is the only truth."

But there was something underneath; not calculation, but heat. I wasn't sure what was worse.

I could have backed out, right then. I didn't. It was a huge risk, but this was too important. "There are missing people. Kira's little sister, Larissa. If she's in that pit, I'm going in. I don't care what any dragons think."

A ripple ran through him, almost invisible: his scales tensed, his claws flexed, his shoulders locked. "Then keep your head." His voice was razor thin. "Inside Ignarath, you can trust no one. Not even me. Or you'll die."

"I wasn't planning on trust," I muttered. "I'm planning on survival."

He looked away, already recalculating routes and weapons, his mind three battles ahead. Fine. I shifted my focus to my own checklist—the only ritual keeping me together. I counted rations, laid out my knife. My hands wouldn't quit shaking; it was adrenaline, not emotion, I told myself. Liar.

The silence between us was savage, thick with night wind and threat. Except now, every time the fire spit, every time he shifted, my body noticed. We were too close. Heat crawled up my spine, soaking beneath my skin, not fear, something else, off-limits and feral.

If it was attraction, I wanted to punch it. If it was terror, even better.

"Dawn, then," I said. I tossed him some jerky we'd managed to salvage. "Eat. I wouldn't want you useless before we get to the suicide part of this journey."

He caught it one-handed. He eyed me like I was another puzzle with teeth. He ate anyway. Something about his jaw, the slow grind, made me shiver. Ridiculous. Grit crunched in my teeth and in my brain.

We sat like that, chewing, every breath a test. Firelight carved his scales into hard lines and shadow. I pretended I was scanning for threats, but really I was keeping him out of my blood. Or trying to.

Eventually, my body gave the order I'd been waiting for. I hunched down. I kept the knife ready. I announced, "You sleep first. Try anything, I'll cut your heart out and roast it on what's left of this fire."

A dry, ugly chuckle came from him, crawling low in his chest. "I would expect nothing less, *veshari*."

I almost asked what that word meant, but I bit my tongue. There was something in Zarvash's gaze daring me to ask. I wouldn't give him the satisfaction.

I meant to keep watch. I meant to stay sharp. Instead, my thoughts circled: Kira's missing sister, Plaktish's sneer, Khorlar's shadow, Zarvash's heat. Every muscle vibrated with too many promises and too little hope. Fear, or hunger, made my skin tight, my breath quick, the space between us electric.

God, what was wrong with me?

I kept my knife in hand, my back to the rock, the last echo of warmth already fading. I waited for the suns and the promises of new danger. The world out there didn't scare me half as much as what crawled under my skin, looking at him, at the space that kept shrinking, no matter how far I tried to run.

There was no going back.

Tomorrow it was Ignarath, and the chance none of us would survive it.

Tonight? Just the two of us, and the fire that I couldn't let die.

IGNARATH'S BORDERLANDS SPRAWLED, wild and pitiless, every shadow a blade, every shimmer of heat a warning. My wing burned; it was a punishment I'd earned, a badge I'd wear until the gods grew bored of my pain. I tuned it out. Weakness was a mouthful of blood, and I spat it.

Vega moved near me, not behind, not truly beside, but in that liminal warzone where equals prowl, always testing the boundary between trust and violence. Her anger was a spill of hot metal, her vigilance riding the edge of a blade. I tasted it in the air as keenly as any enemy's scent.

I wanted her at my back, in my teeth, out from under my skin. It twisted into warning until I couldn't tell the difference.

We slipped through sharp stone and scattered

bones, chasing shade like hunted things, every step another wager against Volcaryth's hate. I logged every detail: the wind's yowl, grit under my claws, the staccato cadence of her breath. The city was close. I could taste it on the wind: smoke, hot iron, and ambition stripped clean of mercy.

She kept her silence, but her eyes carved lines in my skull. Calculating. Turning every possibility until the outcomes bled dry. I stalked ahead, forcing focus, because letting myself look at her, a mistake, every time, would strip flesh from bone and leave only need.

"We hold to the gully." My voice was sand and stone. "The shadows should shield us. If patrols catch us—"

"They'll skin us for boots." Her lip curled, half a sneer, half a cutting smile. "I'm not here to die slowly, Zarvash."

"Neither am I." My tail lashed, anger my only armor. "Keep moving. Quietly. Luck's the only thing we've got left."

Her laugh was knife-edged. "If that's the plan, dig my grave shallow. Don't waste the effort."

I grunted, no warmth in it. "You want a guarantee, find a softer world."

She flung a look at me, sharp, burned-out amusement sparking under the sand, and something in me twisted with it, ugly and unfinished.

Ahead, the land caved into a saddle of blackened bone, crusted by fire. Beyond was Ignarath's skyline, spires like spears stabbed through the world's throat, banners raking the sky so high even the light seemed to bleed.

She stared at the city's edge. Her mouth was all iron, but her fingers flexed like she was already closing them around someone's windpipe. "How do we get past the walls?"

I stopped, jaw locked. My scales itched to move, to drag her away and leave the damn city behind. "Flying's suicide. There are archers all along the walls, and you'll find your wings nailed over the gates for trying to fly in without permission." Not that we could try it with my injured wing.

She wiped sweat from her brow, jaw set hard. "So, we go in the front door?"

"We'll have to try it. But they'll gut you for breathing wrong."

"Figures." She hiked her pack higher. "Going to charm us through?"

"Charm's wasted here." I jerked my chin at the haze over the wall. "They see you, they see fresh meat. They see me, and they see a threat. It doesn't matter. No one's looking for friends."

She moved in my shadow, step for step. "Do you have a trick tucked away? Some secret passage you forgot to mention?"

There was no trick. Only lies. "I'm still thinking." It tasted like dust. I could think of only one way to get Vega into the city, and she wouldn't like it.

Her laugh was a cough, bitter. "Improvising in the wastelands. That's sure to work."

I almost spat something back, but I heard it, a shift in the wind, the drum of beating wings. The world shrank to a blade's width, every sense on a blade's edge.

"Down." My snarl was more threat than word. "Two Ignarath."

She slid her knife out and crouched, eyes narrowed, murder in her stillness.

My mind raced, marking escape and kill-zones. "Stay behind me and put that thing away. They see you, you die. That simple."

She bristled, met my eyes with open defiance, but slipped the knife away again.

The two Ignarath cut across the sky, wings out wide, showing off. The big one had a whip wrapped around his wrist, promising stinging violence.

They landed with a flourish. They weren't wearing guard uniforms, but that didn't matter. Everyone in Ignarath was a threat.

"State your name." The big one's voice was all bark and bone. "You don't belong here. And what's that *thing*?"

It took everything in me not to growl and lunge at them. How *dare* they presume. But I had to play this right.

I dropped my eyes, played the lesser. "I'm a trader. Raiders took my cargo, and this *thing* is all I managed to salvage." I nodded Vega's way but didn't dare look at her. I needed her to trust me, to play along. We could still save this. "They call themselves humans. Aliens from some savage world. I heard the council likes toys."

It tasted like acid and defeat.

The smaller one sneered. "Why not crawl through the east gate, trader?"

"Where do you think I was going?" I let my gaze flick to Vega. She didn't move. "I just wanted one last moment to ... enjoy this thing."

They exchanged a look of disgust.

The little one spat at my feet, and his hand went to his blade, muscles tensed for violence.

I watched his eyes, read the twitch, and barely got a warning out before it erupted.

The big one lunged, whip uncurling from his wrist with a crack that split the air. Sun flashed along its length, and I twisted beneath the lash. The tip caught the edge of my bad wing—pain, fiery and blinding, kicked through every rib. I roared, fueled by spite and adrenaline, and drove forward. My claws found his forearm, wrenched the tender joint with all the hate pent up in me. Something gave with a wet, soiled click. He shrieked and spat broken teeth into my face as his whip tumbled from useless fingers.

His tail lashed low. I took the hit on my knees, legs crumpling for half a breath, hard grit chewing at my scales. I punched upward, claws digging into the chord of his neck, feeling the pulse thudding there, wanting to rip. He swung a fist, catching my cheek, but the blow only dragged me deeper into bloodlust.

Metal hissed. The little one darted for Vega, fast, all sinew and wicked steel. His blade flashed, an arc slicing for her throat. She twisted, rolled with a dancer's beauty, and let him overextend. Her elbow cracked into his ribs. He doubled, and she pivoted, leg sweeping his feet from under him. He hit the ground hard; she followed, driving her blade into his thigh to the hilt.

His scream ripped through the rocks, higher than any war cry. He didn't drop the knife. Vega snarled, teeth bared, and twisted the blade, turning his cry to a bubbling, ragged moan punctuated by curses in Ignarath dialect.

The big one thrashed under me, trying to buck free. I hammered his wrist with my heel until bone crunched. His other hand fumbled for the whip, too slow. I snatched the coil and snapped it across his face, split a scale, tasted his blood on my tongue. He rallied, slammed his skull into mine. Spots burst in my vision, but I clung on, forehead grinding down into his jaw. Cartilage crumpled; he spat blood and bile, face slick and trembling now.

The little one, leg pumping hot blood, went for Vega's eyes with clawed fingers, but she caught his hand, twisting until knuckles turned white. She planted a knee into the meat of his tortured thigh again and again, drawing fresh shrieks from between his chipped fangs. But even wounded, he was Drakarn. His wings flared. Sand exploded into the air, spraying Vega's face as he heaved her sideways and sprung, using the last surge of agony to launch himself out with a broken, lurching flap, wild blood streaking down his leg.

My own enemy bucked beneath me, fury giving him strength, but I locked my claws in the hollow of his neck, pressed until his scales changed color. He gurgled, spat more defiance. "Coward! Traitor—"

"Keep talking," I hissed. "I'll peel your tongue from your mouth."

He stilled, hatred burning in his golden eyes. For a moment, the world held its breath. Vega and I, panting and blood-smeared, Ignarath blood soaking the sand between us, broken bodies steaming in the fierce light.

With one last shove, I slammed his skull against the ground. He stopped fighting. My claws still dug in until I was sure he wouldn't be getting up again.

Vega crouched low, knife ready, watching the one who'd fled become nothing but a smudge on the sky.

Blood dripped off my knuckles, hot and sweet and proof we were still alive.

Her blood hit my nose, thin, metallic, too close. Instinct yanked me toward her, nearly shoulder to shoulder. "Are you hurt?" My voice rumbled, lower than a growl.

She rolled off the stone, breath heaving. "It's just

a scratch." Her palm dug into her shoulder, blood slicking her clothes. "I'm fine."

The urge to check, the need to see, to taste threat or fate, roared in me. I grabbed her arm, rougher than I meant, and held until her eyes locked on mine. The world shrank to her pulse beneath my claws, the heat between us a forge, fever and fear tangled.

She didn't flinch. She held my stare, bared her teeth, a challenge caught somewhere between dare and victory.

She broke it first, voice ground out through dust. "That one's going to sing all the way to the city; we'll have every vulture with scales after us soon."

Cold logic tamped down my urges.

My claws ached as I let go, skin buzzing with the ghost of her. "We need to get into the city fast, before he has a chance to talk."

Her nod was all edge and bite, a predator's snarl back in her eyes. "And have you come up with a plan?"

I ripped my hand away, fingers flexing in the heat. I sifted through the dead Ignarath's satchel, turned out tokens, a council chit, some ragged bit of favor, not enough, not with blood on the sand this fresh.

Our options were ash, every one worse than the

last. "We need to be what they expect to see. Slave and trader. A Drakarn with a leashed pet." The words burned, shame and violence braided tight.

Her eyes went dead black, danger flaring cold and pure. "You just want me to trust that you won't *actually* sell me? I remember the damned mating trials. You've been trying to push humans out of Scalvaris for months! Why the hell should I trust you?"

"No one's selling you." The words were stone. "And whatever my feelings about your presence in Scalvaris, I would not dishonor myself by lying to you. You've saved my life. I owe you a debt."

The air between us buzzed, venom and challenge drawn tight as a nerve. Her jaw flexed under her bruises, eyes daring me, daring the world, to say one wrong word.

"There's the leash, or there's a grave." My voice scraped like broken glass. "No third option. Not with the Ignarath."

Her eyes burned, hot and cold, afraid and furious. She would never kneel, never give in. Not for them.

Not for me.

"Trust me. Play the part. Or we die."

WATER.

It was a cheap excuse, but if I stood next to Zarvash for another minute, I'd punch the words out of his mouth. My shield, my battered ticket to three minutes of breathing room away from that fire-eyed monster.

It was astonishing, really, how a body could ache for relief and risk in exactly the wrong proportions.

I grabbed the scavenged flask and shot Zarvash my deadliest *I hope you swallow a sun-scarab in your sleep* glare. He didn't rise to the bait. One brow arched, that infuriating shade of amusement in his eyes, the kind that said he'd seen every kind of tantrum, dissected it, and found it wanting. My fists curled.

It would be satisfying, deeply, to break a knuckle or two on his stupid, inscrutable face. Maybe that would shake loose whatever weird spell he'd slipped under my skin.

He didn't move. Didn't so much as twitch an ankle to block my path. Smart, maybe. Or, worse, indifferent, except that the glint in his eyes said otherwise. Every second of proximity made my molars grind, a friction born of a thousand cautions and one too many irrational, hot spikes of ... want.

God. Even thinking the word felt like a betrayal.

I stalked off. My wrist pulsed in pain, deep and sharp, not just bruised but a reminder of every mistake since landing on this gods-be-damned planet. I had to ignore it.

I had to disregard Zarvash, his shadow, the way he kept his wings angled just so, his tendency to watch and not interfere, like I was some problem he'd decided to solve only at the last possible moment, as if he could hold himself aloof from the mess of us humans clinging to survival by spite and habit.

*I didn't choose to be here, buddy.*

My mind was a cauldron, bubbling over with poison and the ghost of his touch. Still. That brief sweep of his claws, gentle, somehow, as if he knew how breakable I really was, left heat in my skin and confusion in my blood.

Betrayal, treason at the molecular level; my bones feeling hunger instead of hate.

No. Not him.

Of all the scaled bastards on this hell planet, it had to be Zarvash? Brilliant strategist, stone-cold manipulator, not one ounce of kindness in all that muscle and those rough hands.

It was a great cosmic punchline: Vega Cross, survivor of covert ops, last best hope of Don't Catch Feelings, now getting all tingly for the one Drakarn most likely to sell her for parts, or worse, destroy her on principle.

I kept moving. If I stopped, if I let myself spiral the heat crawling along my every nerve might finally catch and burn me alive. And wouldn't Zarvash just love a show?

The well looked ancient, littered with history: banded stone blackened by more turns of the suns than I cared to count, dusted with the tracks of animals and the faded memory of desperate claws. The wind snapped, dirty with sand, and for a flash, I let myself stand still in its teeth and waited for the blaze in my thoughts to bank.

But of course, Volcaryth didn't allow peace. Not for me. Not for anyone with human skin and too much fight in their blood.

I heard the sound too late, all wrong, heavy, slow. A predator's approach.

And not my predator.

I spun. My knife was ready, except my fingers wouldn't quite close, the pain at my wrist a firework burst behind my eyes. There he was. The Ignarath I'd stabbed—a messy gash at the thigh, still leaking but far less than it should have been. Drakarn healed fast; this bastard seemed to be doing it out of sheer spite.

He grinned.

It was a study in the grotesque: blood-streaked fangs, bruise-colored gums, a tongue that flickered as if testing the taste of my fear in the air. The blood on his leg didn't match the triumph in his step. He circled me, savoring the pulse of my discomfort, and his gaze, oily, bright, raked me from collarbone to calves and back up again.

"The prey has teeth," he rasped, almost admiring. "Not marked yet, are you? Not truly owned." He bared what might have passed as a smile on a bad day, tail flexing in slow arcs through the dust. Every muscle in my body went rigid.

I bared my teeth and wished I had true fangs of my own. "Try me, worm-breath. I'll show you how we do it back home."

The Ignarath's tail lashed too fast, and pain exploded in my hand at my grip as the knife flew, skittering away. Shock, white and hot, ran up my arm, my breath trapping itself between my teeth.

*Too slow, Vega. Much too slow. And now you're dead.*

He was on me, claws at my jaw, filthy scales scraping my skin. I tensed, an old trick, feign a flinch, then headbutt, but he must have sensed it coming because his other hand snapped up, catching my battered wrist in a vise.

Agony knifed through me. Something inside protested, sick and bright. I could feel the world narrowing to a tunnel. My legs were still fucking useful and kicked, aiming low. He grunted, doubled over, but not enough. His grip remained, hate and hunger mixed in his glare.

His claws dragged my chin up, breath sour and alien as he leaned in. "I like strong pets. You'll fetch a fine price or serve me a long time." It was a searing, ugly promise.

I'd kill myself before I knelt for anyone.

I spat a curse and went for his knee with my

own. Contact. He grunted. His tail, thick with muscle, licked out, wrapping my calf and wrenching me sideways. I saw sky, then hard, pitiless sand, my forearm skinning itself in a burning bloom of pain.

I forced myself up, refusing to crawl. If I died, it would be on my feet.

He advanced. Shadows closed tight around me, my own breath hot and ragged in my ears, pain driving out all the leftover heat from Zarvash's touch.

And then the world cracked open.

Zarvash hit us like a meteor, no warning, no sound, just bronze fury incarnate. He tackled the Ignarath with staggering violence, every muscle rigid, restraint burned away. His wings snapped wide, injured, but lethal enough, and the Ignarath was slammed back, claws flailing, a guttural curse scraping the wind.

I watched helplessly, hunched, clutching my wrist to my chest. Zarvash became something new and old. He fought with a savagery a human couldn't imitate, couldn't possibly survive. No wince, no calculation, just action.

He roared in a voice that didn't recognize mercy. It made the air vibrate; even the sand under me hummed.

"You. Do. Not. Touch. Her."

Those words—not a threat, a verdict.

The Ignarath fought like a cornered snake, claws, fangs, tail everywhere. Zarvash matched him blow for blow; his claws found the Ignarath's arm, and with a wet, remarkable crunch that made my stomach lurch, tore through scale and tendon. Blood spattered, sickly sweet and copper, and Zarvash didn't blink. Didn't even care that his own wing dragged stiffly, the wound raw.

I watched a creature made for war; not the cool operator from a distance, but a storm, broken loose. He pinned the Ignarath's legs with his tail, smashed his head into the sand with a methodical violence that would have made the hardest soldier blink. I'd seen fights before—street, ring, battlefield. They all seemed polite compared to this.

The enemy spat blood, hissed, lashed out at Zarvash's throat with his own fangs, desperate now. Zarvash ducked, jaws closing around the Ignarath's throat, not hesitant, not drawn out, just a snap, quick and iron sure. The body stilled, jerked once, and the fight was over.

Holy shit. The silence was a new thing, vast and echoing. My heart beat fast in my chest, but it felt off, as though the world's tempo had doubled then snapped.

Zarvash straightened, breathing ragged, sand and blood caked along his bronze scales, eyes wild—lightning in a bottle, trying to find a way out. And then those eyes swung to me. Direct, unblinking. I couldn't move, didn't dare. Every nerve in my body screamed three things at once: run, fight, surrender. Not to him, not ever.

He stalked my way, each step measured. Each moment a negotiation with whatever primal force he'd barely managed to leash.

He reached out, claws softened now, dragging their edges along the skin of my forearm, testing for breaks or worse, then tracing up, uninvited but not unwelcomed, to the bruised line of my jaw.

I flinched, only fair, only sensible, but he didn't press. Just tilted my face up, his hand so hot it might have branded me, eyes searching for damage, or maybe for permission, or maybe even for forgiveness. I didn't know. I couldn't. I was frozen there under his touch, unable to even think about moving. His thumb swept over the bruise there, lingered long enough for my nerves to make their arguments, long enough for the air to feel thick as syrup.

Neither of us spoke. No need. The world shrank: dust, blood, him, me, the gap between his claws and my skin. His gaze flickered, gold and full of something ancient. He looked at my mouth, back up.

Held. Waited.

It would have been easy, in that breathless moment, to let go. To fall into the gravity between us, to erase all the rules just for one kiss that would have been a total disaster. Some foolish part of me wanted it. Wanted *him*, the freaking alien dragon-lizard who hated humans and had hurt my friends.

The heat was getting to me. That had to be it.

He let his hand drop, claws grazing along my jaw one last time, then moving, careful as a surgeon, to the swelling at my wrist. He prodded, tested, all business now but not unkind. "Lucky," he said, the word ground out like it pained him to speak it. "Nothing shattered. Foolish." His voice was rough, almost fond. It felt like being scolded by fate itself.

I wrenched my arm free. I couldn't just sit there like that. I squared my shoulders, dredged up the last scraps of dignity, and held his gaze with what I hoped looked like steel and not collapse.

"I'll play your part." I hated how my voice wavered at the edges, like I wanted to believe it myself, like the word "slave" tasted just as foul as it felt. "Pet, slave, pawn, it doesn't matter. If it gets us through the gates, I'm whatever you need me to be."

Something flickered in his eyes. I couldn't name it. Drakarn emotions ran deep; they didn't leak out unless you watched for the cracks. He nodded like he was still calculating every possible future before allowing himself to speak.

But all he said was: "So be it."

STEPPING up to the Ignarath gates was like reopening a wound that never finished festering.

The air there stung, heat and dust smeared over burnt sugar, old blood, and that acrid, animal tang I'd never scrub from memory. Every breath brought it back: the sleepless cycles, the violence, the weight of a city that devoured the weak and spat out bone.

I'd been young once and eager to prove myself. After limping my way out of the champion's arena, I had sworn never to come back.

And today, I walked right into its gullet, parading my "alien prize" for all to see. Every set of eyes was a knife, itching for weakness, daring me to forget I was nothing but prey dressed in a predator's skin.

Nothing had changed. The towers still clawed at the scorched sky; sandstone stacked with the haphazard pride of a people who couldn't build a straight wall if you paid them in gold. Banners snapped in the wind, brash and bloodstained, clan marks burned in by generations of grudges. Even decay was defiance here, rot worn like armor. Ignarath didn't bother with modesty. The city would have you worship its hunger or be devoured.

Vega caught the scent of danger, just as I did. Her posture tensed, spine straight, eyes sharp, every line screaming "not slave" even as the satchel strap tied around her wrists displayed submission for the crowd. Not really tight. Just tight enough for show.

Only someone searching for the crack would see the steel behind her mask, the jaw that wouldn't yield, the flick of focus beneath her lashes. Stupidly brave, or bravely stupid. Hard to tell there.

At the city walls, the scrutiny thickened until it pressed against my scales, close and suffocating. Drakarn guards slumped in the shade. I jerked Vega close, hard enough to sell resentment, not possession. This place hated weakness, but it loved a show. And nothing screamed "target" like a warrior from Scalvaris dragging a prize, too bold, too desperate, too haunted.

A guard loomed, wide as a doorway and twice as ugly, blocking sun and hope. Wings drooped in that slow, deliberate way the practiced killers use to draw you in before the bite. He didn't bother with politeness. His inspection began and ended with the commodity he assumed I risked everything for.

He sneered, "State your business. No beggars. No gutter trade."

"Trader," I said. "I was robbed outside the South Divide. All that's left is this creature." I yanked Vega, hard enough for the onlookers but not for her. She stumbled, caught herself, snapped me a glare that could salt fields. "I heard your lot buy rare stock. Pay well for it too, if the rumors are worth half a spit."

I let my tail flick. Nerves, not bravado. Sometimes that got you killed; sometimes it got you a second look.

He snorted, mouth curling with open disdain. "Long way from Scalvaris, soft scale." The words bit hard. A soft scale wasn't a warrior, was barely worth his scales. I itched to show him my claws, but Vega wasn't the only one playing a part.

I gave him the slow shrug of someone with nothing left to lose. "Better than feeding scavengers. Maybe your chiefs want something exotic."

His stare slid over Vega, lingered, teeth bared in a way that made my fists tense. "The council's had their fill of oddities. I saw two more like her in Beast's Quarter."

The words spiked something old and hope-shaped in my guts. I crushed it before it showed. Not now. Not here. "Lost most of my pack to raiders. If those are mine, I'll reclaim them. Where should I look?"

He shrugged heavily, uncaring. "Search the Blood Pits if you plan to sell. Skorai screens the best prizes before the games. Move along."

Ignarath and their tournaments. I liked blood sport as much as any other warrior, but this city took it to an extreme. Long ago, I had tested myself on their sands. I still had the scars from that failure. But I was young then. I had no need to prove myself now. Not to them.

Fighting relief and disgust, I tipped my chin, dragged Vega forward into Ignarath proper. I could feel the city's hunger mounting behind us, anticipation rolling through the streets.

Inside, the stares clawed along my spine. Markets teemed, hawkers and slavers screaming in sharp words and old fears. Drakarn children darted, sharp little terrors, slipping between gamblers and vendors with the natural cruelty of the young. Arrogance and desperation coiled together, fighting for air.

Vega trudged beside me in her makeshift bonds, chin up, eyes burning straight ahead. Every muscle ready for the wrong kind of attention. As if by refusing to shrink she could make the city bow instead.

Crowds pressed close, thick at the plaza where the city prepared for its bloodletting. Arena banners hung limp in the noon heat. Workers hoisted new streamers, their hands stained crimson by old dyes. Vendors hawked memorabilia: stone knives shaped after favored champions, trinkets meant to buy a scrap of another fighter's glory. The air stank of sweat.

Vega took it all in with hungry eyes. "What are they preparing for? I've seen battlefields look less frenzied."

"The Ignarath Champion's Tournament," I said, voice flat as paving stones. "It's an annual spectacle. Warriors come from every territory to battle in the pit. The winner walks away with coin, legend, sometimes a seat at the council's feast. The rest ..." I let the sentence rot at the root.

She didn't miss a beat. "Let me guess. You tried once, got your tail kicked by a lizard with bigger claws?"

The memory stung. I shrugged. "I was knocked out early. I was young and brash."

That earned a noise halfway between a laugh and a snort. "As opposed to how you're so old and calm now?"

We were eyed with the malice this place reserved for strangers. I led us along the edge, skirting the widest crowds, always aware of how easily two could vanish, never to be found.

She scanned the crowd around us like she was looking for the weak link. "We need to find the humans. The ones that guard mentioned."

"We just got here; eyes are watching," I replied. "We need to secure a place to sleep first. We don't want to raise any unnecessary suspicion."

She bristled, set her jaw. "They've been stuck here for months." Her frustration bled through.

"If we move too quickly, we'll fail before we start."

She was silent for three paces, then spoke. "You're not calling the shots here." She held up her hands. "Don't get confused."

I almost smiled but didn't. Not here. "If obeying was your skill, neither of us would be here."

She shot me a filthy look and set her stride again, chin unwavering.

A shadow split the crowd, and suddenly we stepped into a street quieter than the last—crumbling guesthouses hunched between trader dens and gambling holes, paint flaking to expose rock scarred with ancient graffiti. A weathered Ignarath female idled at the nearest door, scales a soft pink. She had hard eyes.

I angled toward her. We needed one night's peace—if Ignarath even remembered the word.

Then a voice like oil over gravel. "Pretty pet you got there, soft scale."

Vega stiffened. The speaker, a gaudy arena enforcer, scales lacquered to a garish shine, chest crisscrossed with leather straps, loomed in our path. He reached with practiced indifference and clamped thick fingers around Vega's arm.

I felt something snap in my chest, fear and fury, knotted together with something like need. For a heartbeat, Vega was all razor instinct, shoulders bunched, eyes wild, murder burning beneath the surface. She let out a sound too wild for a whimper, too raw for a threat, and the crowd stilled, waiting for blood to spill.

Three seconds: I saw the massacre that would follow. If she fought, the crowd would close like a trap. Claws would flash.

Ignarath demanded theater. Let them see a monster, not a victim.

I lunged, stalking past the red haze in my vision, wings flaring in the narrow street, hunger sharpening every word. I ripped the leash taut, glaring death at the brute.

My growl rolled over the street.

"Touch what's mine again, and you'll pay for it in blood, you dog." I dragged Vega closer, hard, baring my fangs. "She's not for pawing. Unless you want to test me, back off. I break things that don't belong to me."

He let go, making a show of carelessness, but I saw his eyes, a flicker of risk, of calculation. Not worth his time. He flicked Vega a final look, ugly with curiosity, then slunk back into the crowd.

But the city was awake now. Whispers swirled. Spectators leaned in, waiting for more.

I gave them what they craved. Yanked Vega up, made a spectacle of control as I barked, "So much as make a sound again, and I'll muzzle you, prey." I squeezed her shoulder, enough for the lookers, not enough for a bruise. I hoped.

Bile rose in my throat at the look of absolute hatred in my—in Vega's eyes.

It shamed me. More than I'd admit. But survival here cost dignity. Vega hissed, fury grinding against necessity, but did not resist. Not now. Not with eyes on us.

I shoved her forward, forced open the guesthouse door. The crowd, denied their violence, drifted away, already sniffing for another feast. I kept close behind her, still scanning for threats.

Inside was a dank, cramped room. Shadows layered atop the rot of sweat and old oil. The proprietor, a Drakarn female scrubbed dull with years, appraised us with a glance. My scars. Vega's bonds. Our exhaustion.

I gave her money we'd taken from the Drakarn who attacked us outside the city, and she slid keys across the desk without question. Up warped stairs we trudged, no words, to a room with one thin window and a door that stuck before admitting us. The single bed would barely be big enough for me.

Only when the bolt clicked shut did the world pause.

Vega whirled, cheeks burning, fists white against the leash. She yanked free and shoved me, hard enough to shake dust from the beams. "What the hell was that? I had it under control; he was nothing."

I let my eyes close, counted out the weight of breaths, forced my heartbeat to slow. Her rage was a sandstorm, mine a desert, silent and abrasive, scraping everything raw.

"I sold the lie we both agreed to. If you moved against him and I didn't strike you down, we'd both be in a cage now. Or worse. With no hope of finding your precious humans."

She glared, massaging her shoulder. "Next time, I break his fingers myself and deal with the mob."

I shook my head. "This place doesn't forgive mistakes."

Vega turned her back, jaw tight, posture flickering between pride and pain. Light crawled in through slats, painting fresh lines over the dingy room.

The silence stretched, tension so thick I could bite it. Her anger filled the room, an electric storm itching to strike. My own pulse thudded heavy, echoing with everything I couldn't afford to name.

I wanted to touch her. To pull her close. My fangs ached. So did my chest. This was the last thing either of us needed, but my entire being cried out to surrender to it.

I'd be a fool to try.

"I'm going to get us something to eat," I said, searching for an excuse to leave her for just a moment, to give me space to breathe.

Vega's glare burned into my wings as the door clattered shut behind me.

OKAY. Deep breaths.

The door clattered shut behind him, the finality vibrating out into the heavy silence. Zarvash. Gone.

For now.

Relief punched through my chest, harsh enough to make my knees threaten to buckle. I took a shaky inhale, filling my lungs with the dirty, dusty air of Ignarath.

Nobody looming, nobody watching, nobody looking at me like they wanted to peel me open and eat my insides.

No Zarvash.

The reprieve was brief. Gone before I'd even finished my first shaky exhale.

Anger hit next. Not a warm, fiery burst, but cold, sharp, the kind that cracks stone. That performance out there, his hands on me, the snarled words for the crowd, "defiant pet" in front of a ring of slaver-eyed bastards, it scraped a layer raw I didn't even know I had.

*Touch what's mine again, and you'll pay for it in blood.*

The memory of his growl throbbed in my skull. Possessive. Threatening. Directed at everyone, except maybe not. Because he'd looked at me when he said it, like I was prey.

No.

He looked at me like I was *his*.

And God help me, the worst part, the part that made me wish for brain bleach, for a way to peel my own skin off and scrub it raw, a small, mutinous coil of heat had burned low in my belly. Not fear, not hatred. Something sideways, embarrassing, something an awful lot like want. Betrayal, from the inside out.

*Get a grip, Cross.*

I started to pace in the dilapidated little room. Three steps. Turn. Three back. The planks shivered, some catching and snagging at the soles of my boots. Splinter, pinch, ignore. Think.

I needed my mind on the same page as my body. Zarvash was Drakarn. Scalvaris's favorite strategist, legendary for his utter lack of trust in anything soft, squishy, or human.

Not my friend, not my ally except by some spectacularly terrible accident of necessity.

He'd nearly gotten Orla killed with his machinations with the Forge Temple. Zarvash's loyalty was only going to last as long as the tactical advantage did. I was an asset. A chess piece. Expendable. His equation had to be: How much is she worth dead? How much alive?

I couldn't trust him. Not deeply, not with my plans. With my life? It was a fool's bargain, but he was the only person I knew there, and anyone else would sell me ... or worse.

That act out there? Pure theater, the sort of thing baked into the bedrock of survival in that suns-poisoned garbage heap of a planet. Nothing personal. It wasn't supposed to feel personal. Except it did. The way his claws had wrapped around my shoulder, possessive, tight, just this side of pain, or the heat that had rolled off him, vibrating with banked violence.

I'd known exactly where I stood: one inch from the teeth, a heartbeat away from being used as a weapon or a shield.

The moment where it felt like he was defending

me? It wasn't real. Couldn't be. Just tactics wrapped up in violence. I hated that a part of me—the dumb, hormonal, lizard-lusting part—had registered something else.

I glared down at my wrists. Red, swollen, angry where the strap was biting in. I fumbled at the knot, fingers half-numb and clumsy. The thing was stubborn. I yanked, swore, and yanked even harder. Of course the bastard hadn't thought to untie me before he ran the fuck away.

The knot finally gave, the restraint falling to the ground. I kicked it across the room with a tight jerk of my leg. The relief stung. I flexed my hands, shook them out, rubbing at the sensitive places that were almost bleeding. A reminder of how bad this could all go.

Dust motes, slow-motion, spun in a lone blade of filthy sun slicing through crooked shutters. Everything smelled like sweat and old metal and the ghosts of blood and old fucking. The centerpiece of the décor: one bed. More a slab, barely wide enough for Zarvash's wingspan, half-covered in a blanket that looked something close to clean. I didn't want to get close enough to give it a sniff.

My stomach cramped, that distinct edge of hunger making itself known. Where was Zarvash?

Part of me wanted him to vanish forever and let me figure this mess out solo. It simplified the math. But the practical, unkillable survival part knew better. Getting whatever humans we could find out of Ignarath would require Zarvash.

Just setting foot in the city had been like jamming my tongue in acid. The tension there was different, meaner, broader than Scalvaris's honest echoing danger. Scalvaris was shadowed, claustrophobic, but it didn't hide anything in those shadows. Ignarath was a wound left open under twin suns, all blood and teeth and who could bite deeper.

You walked in, and you were evaluated, weighed, flayed alive by a dozen watching eyes: predator or prey, asset or waste.

I'd hated the caves. But now? Scalvaris was starting to look like home.

Here? The way that guard had stared at me, cold calculus. The slaver's look—what can I get for her, and how much pain can she take before it's too much work? Even pretending, it soaked in. The powerlessness. Didn't matter if I'd signed up. I wanted to burn that humiliation out of my bones.

Were the others looking for me? Hawk, Terra, Selene? Had they already marked me as dead, written my name on a gravestone and moved on? And then there was Kira. I hoped she wasn't blaming herself. My mistake. My overreach, my need for answers, my faith in my abilities at the worst possible moment.

Damn it.

The ache in my stomach was starting to bother me when the door rattled. My hand shot to the knife strapped at my calf, muscles tensed tight. But it was Zarvash. Even seeing his familiar form, it took me several seconds to calm down.

He stepped in, filling the doorway: shadow and scale, tired eyes. Just a man, or dragon monster, and not at his best. I saw it, the bronze of his scales streaked with city dust, the slump in his left wing, injury hidden but not gone. He was running on fumes. Just like me.

He had a bundle in one clawed hand, steam rising, food smell laced with a tang of oil, and a battered waterskin hanging at his side. He didn't say anything, just gave a nod at the miserable excuse for a bed, then dropped the food onto its threadbare blanket.

I didn't argue. My dignity had already moved out. I sat, tested the edge of the slab, half-worrying it might collapse under me. But Drakarn preferred stone sleeping platforms, and this was as hard as I'd come to expect.

Zarvash dropped down at the end. Proximity: suddenly way too much. The room shrank by half.

He unwrapped the bundle. Steam—hot, spicy, meaty—rose into the stagnant air. Dumplings. Delicious. He offered one, a lean across the too-short gulf. My fingers brushed his as I took it. His scales were cool. I pretended not to notice the shiver knifing up my arm.

We ate, silent, watching each other across the DMZ of our sleeping platform. Tense, calculating silence. Like sharing a foxhole with someone who might, or might not, shoot you when this was over. I stared at the food, chewed slowly.

Don't think about the alien sitting three feet away. Don't think about arm muscles under his torn tunic. Focus on survival.

He finished first, wiped his mouth with the back of his scaled hand. Efficient, but not pretty. His gaze dropped in a way that set every alarm in me screaming, straight to my wrists, the ugly red welts left from the staging. I pulled them away, too slow. He saw.

A growl started low in his chest. Before I could brace, he'd reached out, one huge hand swallowing my left wrist. My entire body went electric, every nerve sparking, adrenaline surging. Reflex screamed: yank away, grab the knife.

I didn't move.

His claws, curved and lethal, ghosted over my pulse point. I could feel the throb of my blood, erratic and panicked. And something else I *really* didn't want to name.

"Hold still," he ordered.

I wanted to jerk back on principle. To tell myself I was still the one in control here. But my body had other plans.

He uncorked the waterskin, fingers deft and surprisingly graceful for hands so lethal. A slip of wet cloth pressed gently and slowly against my wrist. Careful, precise, as if I were some rare, breakable specimen. Not a prisoner. Not prey.

I shuddered. Heat prickled under my skin. It burned up my arm, haze and static, nerves twanging in time with my pulse. Every touch was a new spark. I resented it. Relished it. Didn't know where to put the wanting.

He paused, gaze boring into the space where my flesh rose, small shivers, betraying me with every shallow breath. His thumb brushed deliberately over the goosebumps. Almost wonder, something like hunger flickered in his eyes, raw and unguarded, so unlike the calculating strategist I'd catalogued and hated and, God help me, noticed.

"Your skin. It rises. Why?" The words vibrated out of him, low and heavy, close enough to melt into my bones. Not scornful. Curious. Hungry. Like the puzzle of me had him absolutely riveted.

A claw danced its way up my arm, feather-light and agonizing, tracing a map of heat and blood. Each graze left a pulse behind, tight, electric, intimate. My body arched to it for half a second before I caught myself, but he saw.

Of course he saw.

My breath caught, turned ragged. Not fear, I recognized that old, animal instinct. This was something more slippery, more dangerous. Dread and desire, tangled and indistinguishable in the moment. I tried for science, for analytic distance. I failed spectacularly.

I wasn't just being handled; I was being studied. Admired and consumed by his focus. Under that stare, I wasn't less. I was too much. Nerve endings overloaded, skin tuned to his frequency, every instinct in me screaming: Yes. Yes. Don't you dare stop.

He leaned in, an invasion, heat radiating off him like a furnace. The air thickened, crackled. His scent wrapped around me: dust, stone, and something wild, base, beautiful. I could taste it, could almost taste him.

His head dropped, lips parted, hovering just above my skin, close enough I could feel the heat of his breath, the promise strung taut between us.

Not prey. Not an experiment. No, not for a second.

I should have pulled away. Should have said something sharp, driven a wall up between his want and mine. But my body was honest, traitorously honest, urging closer, arching into his orbit, breath coming quick and wanting.

The danger wasn't that he'd break me.

The danger was that I'd say yes.

He sat there, studying me like something half-wild, half-sacred. Like he couldn't decide if he wanted to conquer me or worship me. I held his gaze, chin up, defiant but shaking, inside, anyway. Refusing to give him the satisfaction of seeing how badly I wanted to close the distance.

The silence vibrated. Breathless. Heavy.

He went lower, gaze fixed on the chaos at the pulse under my jaw. Then, God and rot and every broken thing, his tongue flicked out. Long, dark, deadly. One slow, deliberate swipe across my wrist, burning and startling and weirdly, breathlessly intimate.

I froze. Blank. Sound dropped away. The world, for one long, vertigo-laced heartbeat, constricted to nothing but the damp heat on my skin, the thought of his alien taste, the wild, unspooling panic and thrill tangled at the root of my spine.

Then he was gone, pulling back like a shutter slamming down, intensity vanishing behind emotional armor.

"You should rest." Flat. Command. Dismissal.

He rose, every movement efficient, practiced, distant. He parked himself at the fractured window, staring out at the slice of sky hacked between the filthy buildings.

My body was still locked up, perched on the edge of the bed, hands trembling, skin tingling with the echo of that tongue. Mind racing. Trying and failing to box away what just happened, index and file it like a fever dream.

But control had left the building. Something vital and dangerous had cracked open between us, transgression leaking into every breath, every nerve. We'd crossed a line I hadn't even seen, the ground underfoot suddenly all trapdoors and razor wire.

And the ugliest truth, the one I didn't want to

touch? I didn't know if I wanted to find my footing again.

This was bad. So freaking bad.

I stared at the scarred shutters, jaw set, heart trying to burrow straight through my ribs. Rest, he'd said. Like I could. Like that was possible in this world, this body, with this new, unnamable ache singing under my skin.

God damn it.

7

VEGA

SLEEP? Not tonight. I managed maybe twenty minutes before every inch of my body shot electric with warning, fingers curled around my knife. It had slithered under the torn hem of a blanket. My breath caught, and for a wild second, I half-expected to see an alien claw descending or some Ignarath freak busting through the door.

But it was just the room, our sad little splinter of sanctuary. Zarvash sprawled on the bed, motionless except for the rise and fall of that too big chest. In the dimness, he looked less like a dangerous warrior and more like the monster I'd imagined under my bunk as a kid. The one with claws, fangs, and a bottomless void for a heart.

I'd made him take the bed. Like an idiot.

After that skin-hot moment earlier, his claws

ghosting over my wrist, that tongue, God, that unexpected scorch of his touch, even thinking about
sharing the bed was absolutely out of the question.
And he still needed to baby that wing if he was ever
going to fly us out of there. So, I'd staked out a patch
of cold wood in the corner and pressed my spine to
the wall like that would hold me together.

Outside, laughter crashed through the night,
drunken, furious, and feral. Somewhere nearby,
something heavy hit the dirt, followed by the painful
sound of bone or maybe teeth connecting with something alive. My brain ticked through every noise,
instant threat assessment, cataloging: safe, dangerous,
maybe both.

Sleep never stood a chance. But that wasn't even
the problem.

It was the ghost of a memory haunting my skin,
the soft, terrifying press of Zarvash's claws on my
flesh. Gentle, somehow, in total defiance of my
expectations. His tongue, quick and ... fucking
precise, soothing the rawness on my wrist. But
searching, too, like he could taste my fear, my confusion, the chaos roiling just under the surface. And
the forbidden fucking want.

I did *not* need this.

I pushed my palms against the rough, grit-scabbed floor, tried to let the cold crawl inside my overheated body. "Get a grip," I mouthed, barely breathing.

This wasn't one of Terra's clandestine stares at Darrokar. Not Orla, moon-eyed for Rath, or Selene with Vyne. Least of all Hawk, giving Khorlar those sharp, hungry looks when she thought no one was paying attention.

If it was, I'd owe Hawk one hell of an apology.

But it wasn't.

I'd torn into Hawk last time. Hadn't pulled a damn punch. Accused her of letting her judgment slip, mocked her for drooling over scaly muscles with our people still lost out there.

And now there I was, pulse stuttering whenever a dragon-monster in strategist's armor let his gaze linger a beat too long.

Pathetic.

The bar crowd erupted outside. My nerves shot into high gear and then calmed once I realized it wasn't for me. For a simmering second, I wondered if I'd survive the night without Zarvash's shadow between me and whatever prowled the alleyways.

The window glared down at me, flimsy wooden shutters, one loose on its nail, promising escape or maybe just another brand of death. Beyond that? A city slavering for blood, for the spectacle of soft-fleshed captives torn apart. But also ... maybe, maybe, Kira's sister or any human someone I'd promised myself I'd find, back before I hitched myself to the slumbering monster in the bed.

The guilt was a stone, cold and relentless, grinding under my breastbone. I'd heard the rumors. Known what was at stake. And there I was, locked up in a room with a Drakarn, counting my heartbeats, too scared to move, too furious to sleep.

My wrist ached, still tingling where Zarvash's breath and tongue had touched it, the sensation flickering between a warning flinch and something I wasn't about to put words to. Too much fear, too much need, too much everything balled tightly under my skin.

Across the room, Zarvash didn't stir. That wounded wing was a dark scythe, folded clumsily, vulnerable for once. Back when I'd patched it up, he hadn't so much as growled. But it had to be hurting him.

And if I stayed in that room another second, I might do something stupid like try and soothe it.

I should wake him. Say I was going for air. The smart move, the safe move.

I didn't.

Instead, I uncoiled, every joint protesting the cold, the stress, the wrongness. I'd cataloged the language of the floorboards: third from the door squeaks, fifth sags, skip both. Knife, always, back in its sheath.

The click of the latch sounded like gunfire. Zarvash didn't so much as sigh; dead to the world or just letting me think so.

Six feet from freedom, or at least from breathing room.

The hall was pure blackness, sliced with sick-yellow lantern light from somewhere far below. I jammed my feet into my boots, forced numb fingers to work laces until they were tight enough to run, tight enough to feel like armor.

Running from what? Ignarath, its claws out. Zarvash, if he woke angry. Or worse, running from this thing worming under my ribs, this sick pinch of guilt and something rougher, hotter. I had to move.

Creak. Step. Creak. Every bone in the flophouse joined in, as if warning the city. Nobody yelled. Only the revelry outside answered, echoing up the stairwell.

At the foot of the steps, the entryway was abandoned. The main door hung on crooked hinges. Of course it wasn't locked; what idiot would try to break in there? All the danger was already inside.

Night air was a slap, cool, sharp, chasing sweat from my temples. The moon bled over unfamiliar roofs, making the city feel even more alien and predatory, as if it was waiting for someone to let down their guard. Shadows huddled under doorways. The main drag was a party—Drakarn jammed elbow-to-elbow around a makeshift pit in front of the tavern, all teeth and shouting, tossing something like dice or bits of bone into the center.

As the crowd parted, I caught sight of the battleground: two pitiful animals, their scales fever-red, battered and scrambling in a spray of sand and spit. When one got the upper hand, claws locking tight, pinning colored wings, the mob shrieked their approval.

Of course. No matter how far you fly from Earth, throw enough bodies together, and someone will start a cock fight.

No one saw me. No one even glanced my way. I drifted through the shadows, keeping close to stone walls, every sense straining, watching for claws, watching for the cold eyes that might recognize prey.

Every step away from the room, from Zarvash and

safety, made me feel even more guilty. I should have woken him, shouldn't have walked away like that. Should have left a note, a warning, something. But I was already outside now; there was no use turning back.

The market square, abandoned now, was worse than in daylight: limp banners tangled, vendor stalls empty, strips of old cloth that were stained with something I didn't care to examine.

For a wild heartbeat, I let myself pretend this was just a dusty city, ugly, but survivable. For a second, I saw tall towers and yellow cabs and the lights of home. I almost let myself pretend. Almost.

But that wasn't why I was there, and pretending would only get me hurt.

If I was a gladiator or a slaver bragging about prizes, where would I be?

The answer was obvious. Banners snapped northward on the night breeze, marking the route to what looked like half stadium, half execution ground. No grace to it, just hunger, all broken archways and timber, yawning wide as any earthen grave.

I stood there, the weight of my body saying turn back, turn back, but my brain locked on the memory of Kira's voice, her desperation, the ugly possibility of that final loss, and I forced my feet forward.

Inside was worse. The air tasted like pennies and

rot. Benches climbed in ragged tiers overhead, watching, waiting. Moonlight and whatever passed for bleach there warped the sand a sick, flickering shade of silver.

I hugged the wall, refusing to let the idea of being watched claw into my spine, eyes peeled for doors, shadows, secret passages, anything that'd ring as "prison" to a dirty, blood-hungry society.

A door stood out, iron, banded, deliberate. Hiding something. Was this too easy, too obvious? I reached for the latch, then—

Voices.

Not gravel and smoke. Not Drakarn.

Human. Sharp, tired, pissed-off English.

"... can't be serious ..."

"... have a choice?" A second, low and broken.

I slipped closer, heartbeat shoving against my ribs hard enough to bruise. The corridor bent, tunneled toward a grate built for keeping things— people—in. Iron bars, rusted and sturdy. Behind them: shadowy figures. Three. Huddled and ragged.

The pacing one wore what was left of a NASA T-shirt, logo half-obscured by blood and dirt. The recognition was a punch straight to the solar plexus.

They were who I was looking for.

But only three?

I didn't waste another heartbeat on silence. I moved forward, pressed both hands to the cold, rough bars, blood roaring in my ears.

"Hey." My voice was rough with everything I'd been holding in. "Hey, over here."

Three faces jerked towards me, hollow-cheeked and wild-eyed. The one with the cropped hair, a woman, taller than me, face carved in hard lines of exhaustion and disbelief, shot toward the bars, all raw-edged aggression.

"Who the hell are you?" she hissed.

I WAS GOING to kill her when I found her. If the damned Ignarath didn't do it first.

Vega's scent—damn her—cut through the reek of Ignarath. Sweat, blood, and something distinctly *human*, too sweet for this viper's pit. It pulled me, a sickeningly insistent thread, through the warren of winding streets. Past gambling dens where Drakarn tossed knucklebones, laughter like rocks grinding against each other.

The arena district loomed. A monument to savagery, its sloping walls clawing at the bruised moonlight. Torches flickered, casting long dancing shadows. Each step closer was a risk, each breath a taste of the enemy.

My wing throbbed. A constant reminder of my frailty. Alone, wounded, deep in Ignarath territory.

The outcome wouldn't be a question; it would be a butcher's display.

Vega slipped through a shadowed side entrance, moving like a snake herself. Silent. Deadly. She'd slipped from our room like a phantom, no word, no warning. Fury burned like acid in my gut.

Did she have any sense? Every step deeper into this nest ratcheted up the danger. I should have seen this coming. That human ... impulsive, reckless. Exactly the kind of maddening determination that made them impossible to predict. How many times had she done this already in Scalvaris? She should have been caged. Hobbled.

And yet ...

I edged closer, hugging the shadows where torch-light couldn't reach. The arena's underbelly was a maze of stone and iron, designed to hold beasts and gladiators alike, before they were tossed to the screaming sands. Guards patrolled, their talons clicking on stone, tails dragging with bored malice.

Vega moved like she knew the place. Pausing at intersections, checking lines of sight. Caution ... admirable, if not so bloody foolish. I tracked her movements, marking each guard, calculating trajectories. How fast could I reach her if it went to hell?

She vanished around a corner. A curse ripped

from my throat, silent but savage. Moving closer was madness, but staying there ... I slipped from the shadows, wings tight against my back, and followed her scent.

A voice. Not Drakarn. *Human.*

I didn't understand the words, but I guessed the speaker. Female. Wary. Defiant.

Understanding slammed into me. Of course. Not just blind recklessness. She was hunting her people. The guard's words at the gate, replaying in my mind. *Slaves ... Humans ... Arena ...*

I pressed against the wall, close enough to peer around the corner. The corridor opened into a wider chamber. Iron bars stretched from floor to ceiling, caging shadows. Vega stood before them, gripping the metal, her posture coiled and tense.

Three figures huddled in the darkness. Human. Marked by that alien softness. One stepped forward, tall female, hollow cheeks, cropped hair, her stance defiance carved in bone.

They spoke briefly in words I couldn't understand. But they weren't quiet, and sound carried through those damned passageways.

Four Ignarath rounded the corner with a fifth, in leather armor, leading them. An arena officer. They saw Vega instantly and spread out, cutting off escape.

"Well, well." The officer's voice was a dry rasp. "A stray pet, wandering where it shouldn't."

Vega backed away from the cell, hands raised, posture primed for violence. Her eyes darted around. Calculating. Seeking a way out. Finding nothing.

"That's not ... I'm not ..." Her voice quivered, and it was nothing like I was used to hearing. She was playing her role, even there. Even when I could make out the outline of a knife under her tunic.

The officer laughed. Bone-chilling. "All soft-skins are pets. Or food." A gesture to his warriors. "Take it."

They surged forward. Too many. Too fast. Vega ducked the first, elbowing him in the gut. The Ignarath grunted, doubled over. But the others ... They seized her. Grabbing her arms, twisting them behind her back.

She fought. Gods, how she fought. A wild thing caught in a trap. Twisting, kicking, a whirlwind of fury. But she was outnumbered. Overpowered. One warrior struck her. A brutal blow across the face. Her head snapped sideways. Blood welled at the corner of her mouth.

Something inside me shattered.

I stepped from the shadows. Wings flared, and in that moment, I didn't feel the pain of my broken wing, filling the corridor. Neck arched. Fangs bared. Pure dominance. Pure threat.

"Release her." My command was harsh. Absolute.

The Ignarath froze. Their grip slackened just enough for Vega to wrench free. The officer turned, his expression sliding from surprise to contempt.

"Another trespasser." His tongue flicked out, tasting the air. "And this one smells like the soft scales in Scalvaris. What brings you to our arena, outsider?"

I advanced, each step measured. Keeping my gaze locked on his. Dominance was as much about belief as brute strength. "That slave belongs to me." Saying the words was bile on my tongue.

The officer's eyes narrowed. "Strange. She wears no collar, no mark. And she roams unauthorized."

"She wasn't unauthorized." A growl rumbled in my chest. "She was sent. By me."

"Sent?" Skepticism dripped from the word. "For what purpose?"

I drew myself up, summoning arrogance like armor. "I intend to enter your tournament. The creature was gathering information. Assessing the competition, the layout, the opportunities." A baring of teeth. "She has ... unique skills. Valuable insights."

The officer circled, his warriors holding Vega. Her eyes burned into mine. Fury, fear.

*Don't make this worse.* I only hoped she could read my expression.

"You claim to be a warrior," the officer said. "Yet you send a slave to do your work? Cowardice is not valued in our arena."

"Tactics," I corrected. Smooth as death. "Only a fool walks in blind." A flick of my gaze to Vega. "She was supposed to be *discreet.*"

The officer stopped, close enough to smell his breath. Meat. Something rotten. "You expect me to believe this? That you, some worthless trader, would enter our games?"

So, news of our arrival hadn't gone unheard. Rumors spread even faster in Ignarath than they did back home.

"I don't care what you believe." I met his stare, unflinching. "I swear by the Forge I sent her. And I intend to enter your tournament at first light."

A murmur rippled through the warriors. A Forge oath. Not given lightly. Bound by honor, torture, death. Even Ignarath respected that.

Something deep inside me twinged at the lie. Once, not very long ago, I had been a strong follower of the Forge Temple and all they believed in. Those beliefs had been tested, nearly broken. But a life devoted to that creed couldn't be forgotten easily.

The officer's scales rippled in unease. "Bold words. Perhaps to save your pet from punishment." He gestured to Vega. "Rogue slaves are executed. Publicly. Sport before the main event."

I stepped closer. Nose to nose. "Touch what is mine," I growled, voice a promise of pain, "and I will rip your throat out with my teeth."

He didn't flinch, but his pupils contracted. Fear, quick and primal. "Big threats for an outsider."

"Not threats," I said. "Promises. Harm her, and vengeance will echo through your bones long after your scales turn to dust."

He stepped back, reassessing. "Very well. I'll hold your pet for the night. Safe in our cells." A cold smile. "Tomorrow, when the tournament rolls are called, I expect to see your name. If not ..." He glanced at Vega. The threat, clear as a blade.

"She dies before the crowd. A fitting start to the games."

My claws flexed. The urge to tear him apart. Contained. Just barely. I kept my voice level. "I'll be there."

The officer nodded. "Take her to the holding

cells. The secure ones." He turned back. "Prepare, Scalvaris. Our tournament is not known for mercy."

They dragged Vega away. Her resistance renewed. Her eyes locked on mine. A message I couldn't grasp. Fear, yes. Anger, definitely. But beneath it ... trust? Hope? Or just resignation?

"Zarvash ...," she called before a hand clamped over her mouth.

The corridor emptied. Leaving me with the echo of her voice. And the officer's final warning: *Dawn. Or your pet dies screaming.*

I remained motionless until their footsteps faded. Until I was sure. Only then did the mask fall. Rage bubbled. Chained but threatening to break free.

That guard would die. They would all die. For touching her. For threatening her. For daring to believe they could take what was mine.

*Mine.*

The word pulsed. Blood. Bones. Teeth. A truth I could no longer deny. Inconvenient. Impossible. The mate bond sang between us. Invisible, undeniable. Growing with each breath.

I paced beneath the arena's banners. Mind racing. The tournament was a death trap. My injured wing, a crippling disadvantage. But choice was an illusion.

I had to fight. Win. Free Vega. Without getting us killed.

All while battling that bond. That maddening pull. That *mine* that threatened to unravel everything.

I turned back toward the inn. Steps heavy with purpose. Tomorrow would bring blood. Pain.

It would not, however, bring Vega's death. I swore it. On everything I was.

The guard's threat echoed. *Dawn. Or your pet dies screaming.*

Dawn, then. And may the gods have mercy on anyone who stood in my way.

THE IGNARATH GUARD'S FILTHY, hooked talon scraped my neck as he shoved me. Hard. I stumbled, boots skidding on slime-slick dirt, but caught myself. No way was I giving the bastard the satisfaction of seeing me fall. The cell door slammed shut behind me with a final, echoing *thump* that vibrated through the stone and my teeth.

"Enjoy your new home, pet." The guard's sneer stretched his scaled face, yellow eyes lingering like dirty fingers. Malice dripped off him. "Your master better show tomorrow. Or the arena gets a new screamer." He grunted, a wet, satisfied sound, and finally, his heavy footfalls faded down the corridor.

Only then did I let myself breathe. Air thick with old blood, piss, and the sour tang of fear-sweat hit the back of my throat. My jaw pulsed, a deep ache where one of them had clocked me. I tasted blood, copper and sharp, inside my cheek.

Alive. Check.

Functional? Jury was still out.

The cell was a pit. Damp in ways I didn't want to think too hard about. A waste bucket in the corner, radiating its own special stink. Degradation by design.

And eyes. Staring from the shadows. Five pairs. Human.

My heart did a sick little flip-flop, then pounded against my ribs like it wanted out. Gaunt faces. Hollowed-out eyes that held less life than ghosts. Hunger, yeah, but something else. Resignation. That flat, dead look that comes after hope gets ripped out too many times. Three women, two men. Earth clothes shredded to rags. Bodies like stick figures draped in bruises.

"Who the hell are you?"

The voice was rough gravel scraped over stone. It belonged to a woman standing protectively before the others. Dark hair hacked short, eyes narrowed, sharp with suspicion. It was the same question the woman in the other cell had asked, but harder, and somehow more resigned.

I pulled myself straighter, ignoring the sharp

protest from my ribs. "I'm Vega Cross. I'm here to rescue you."

And some job of that I was doing.

The words just hung there in the stale, stinking air. Nobody moved. No cheers, no relief. Just that sharp-eyed stare, dissecting me. Was I hallucinating? A liar? Some new Ignarath mind-fuck?

"Rescue?" A softer voice, cracked with disuse. Hope flickered, fragile as a candle flame. A woman with olive skin, faded magenta streaks clinging stubbornly to strands of black hair, took a hesitant step forward. "How? Were you on the *Nostos*?"

"Yes." I kept my voice low, trying to sound reassuring, even as my own guts churned. "I was in a sleeping pod that crashed near Scalvaris. Another Drakarn city. They're ... different."

Different. Christ, what an understatement.

But asking about the *Nostos* meant these were exactly the humans I was looking for. We'd all crammed into those sleeping pods and surrendered our fate to a ship and an unknown future on some human colony in far off space. It wasn't supposed to be *there*, but we were alive, and that was what mattered at that moment.

A bitter laugh choked out from the corner. A man, slumped against the far wall like his bones couldn't hold him up. "Different? These scaly bastards are all the same. Use you 'til you break, then eat the pieces."

Maybe. I still had my own doubts about the Drakarn. But right then? Survival mode. I moved deeper into the cell, scanning. Automatic threat assessment. A lock as big as my fist. No picking that and, besides, I didn't have tools. Bars thick, rusted but solid. Stone walls looked depressingly sound. Built to hold monsters. Or make them.

"I'm getting us out," I said. A promise that felt heavy, maybe impossible, but necessary. "What are your names?"

*Zarvash, you better show up in the morning.* I had to banish the thought. He would be there. He had to be.

They traded looks. That silent language of shared suffering.

"Kinsley." The first woman, the sharp-eyed one. "This is Nat." Angular features, lean build, coiled tension. "Yelena." The magenta streaks. "Eli." The bitter laugher. "And Asif." A thin man with kind eyes that looked tragically out of place there, gave a tiny nod.

"How long?" I asked, folding myself onto the

gritty floor. Trying not to think about what I was sitting in.

"How long do you fucking think?" Kinsley spat. She still had life in her, still had enough fire to be angry. Good. "Our pod crashed out here. We didn't even have time to figure out which way was up before *they* found us."

"What did they do to you?" I regretted the question even as the words came out of my mouth. Reika had escaped this terrible place and couldn't say a word about it. How could I expect it of people still living in hell?

Nat's mouth twisted. A nerve touched. "We're slaves. We clean the arena after the fights. Serve the warriors." Her voice dropped, roughened. "Whatever they want." That last bit hung there, heavy and ugly. My stomach clenched tight.

"Is a woman named Larissa here?" I leaned forward, pulse picking up speed. "Younger, Asian. Larissa Chen. Her sister, Kira, is in Scalvaris. Safe and alive."

There was a flicker of recognition across Kinsley's face. Thank fuck. "Larissa ... Yeah. They took her somewhere else. Outside the city."

"Why?" The word shot out, too sharp. Damn it. Of course it wouldn't be easy. Not that *this* was easy.

"I don't know." Kinsley hugged her knees tighter. "She knew things. Engineering stuff. One of their officials got real interested."

Air rushed back into my lungs. Alive. Larissa was alive. Kira needed to know. *If* I got back to tell her. A new weight settled. What were they making her do?

"Have you seen Reika?" Yelena asked, voice trembling, hope making her look almost young again. "She was in our pod. Did you ...?"

"Yes," I said, and a real smile, small but there, touched my lips. "She's escaped; she's safe."

The words crashed over Yelena. Hands flew to her mouth, tears instantly welling, spilling over. "Safe," she whispered, the word dissolving into a choked sob.

"How'd you end up in here?" Asif asked. Quiet voice, steady gaze.

I scrubbed a hand over my face. There was grit under my nails. "I came looking for more humans. After we found Reika, we knew you were out here. Then the Ignarath snatched me outside of Scalvaris. The opportunity to investigate was too good to pass up." Not that there was a choice, considering the long hike home Zarvash and I had ahead of us.

If he came.

He would come.

"Alone?" Eli's eyebrows shot up. "Sounds like a suicide mission."

Shit.

How to explain Zarvash? Tell these people, broken by Drakarn cruelty, that one of *them* was my backup? That he might be walking into this shithole arena to get me out? That the thought of him facing those Ignarath butchers made something cold curl in my gut? Fuck.

But I couldn't lie. Not that I was incapable of it— I'd lied myself out of too many situations to count. But it would break their trust right then when I needed it most.

I couldn't have that.

"I wasn't the only one captured by the Ignarath," I said carefully. "There's a Drakarn with me. Zarvash."

Silence. Thick. Heavy. Hostile.

"You're *working* with them?" Nat's voice was pure ice. Disgust plain on her face. "Willingly?"

"It's complicated," I bit out. Understatement of the damn millennium. "Scalvaris, it's ... they're not these Ignarath scum. The gave us shelter. Protection."

"For what price?" Eli challenged, face hardening into granite skepticism.

Terra and Darrokar. Orla and Rath. Selene and Vyne. Hawk and Khorlar. They all flashed through my head. The bonds. Unexpected. Unavoidable. The way we'd woven ourselves into their world or maybe got caught in their web.

*That* I couldn't say a word about. Working with the Drakarn was one thing. Fucking them? None of these humans could understand it. Hell, I didn't understand it.

Until I remembered the gentle feel of Zarvash's claws on my skin. The way his eyes I had lit with an inner fire when he looked at me, when he drew his hands up my arms while I broke out in goosebumps. While I silently wished he'd do more even as I dreaded it.

"Partnership," I said finally. "We help them, they help us."

Nobody looked convinced. Couldn't blame them. Their "partnership" involved cleaning blood off sand.

"This Scalvaris," Kinsley said. "Tell us about it."

So, I did. The underground city, the river. Training grounds. Healing caves. The crash and almost everything that came after it. I skipped the mate bonds. That was too much. Too unacceptable for people living this nightmare.

I watched their faces while I talked. Hope, quickly buried. Wariness. Disbelief. But behind it all, a desperate hunger for *anything* better than that cell.

"How are you planning on getting out?" Nat asked when I finished, blunt and practical. "Unless your Drakarn friend brought an army, forget it."

I hesitated. "He's entering the tournament. We, uh ..." Fuck, they weren't going to believe this part. "They think I'm his slave. I'm collateral. Some guards caught me sneaking around." And Zarvash had to be furious about me sneaking off.

*He'll come.*

"And you trust this guy?" Asif asked.

"Yes," I snapped before hesitation could sell me out. I had to trust him. At least tonight.

Five pairs of eyes looked at me with something like pity. They'd learned over and over again that you couldn't trust Drakarn. And there I was, in a cell with them, telling them that I was letting one of the monsters pretend to own me in an impossible plot to break these people out.

I'd be giving me a pitying look too.

"Sleep," Kinsley said finally, her voice flat. "They do rounds soon, and they'll come in and cause trouble if we're making noise. They don't like it when we speak English."

They didn't have translators. Of course, how could they? That was another problem for the morning.

Sleep. Right. Like my brain would shut off. Like the images wouldn't play on repeat.

I found a spot against the wall, away from the bucket, and drew my knees up tight. Cold stone leeched heat through my clothes, a constant, draining chill.

The others found their corners. A practiced ritual of finding oblivion in misery. Their breathing soon evened out into shallow, wary rest, not real sleep.

Not me. My mind was racing. A hamster wheel of worst-case scenarios.

Zarvash in the arena. Injured wing painting a target on his back. Ignarath closing in. Blood. His death. Mine.

Or maybe he wouldn't show. He could calculate the odds. A strategic retreat. Cut his losses. It made sense. Logical. Smart.

But he'd sworn. *By the Forge.* And that look in his eyes when they grabbed me ... Fury, yes. Raw, blistering fury. But something else underneath. Something that kicked my pulse into overdrive whenever I let myself think about it.

I closed my eyes and saw him. Bronze scales glinting. Those intense gold eyes. The way his tongue had flicked out, tasting my wrist, my fear, my pulse back in that room ...

What the *hell* was wrong with me?

Months spent fighting this. Watching my friends fall into these alien traps. Terra. Orla. Selene. Hawk. I'd warned them. Raged at them.

Now *me*? Pulse jumping at the memory of his touch? Sick with worry about him fighting? *Trusting* him to come?

Alien pheromones? Stockholm syndrome? Just plain stupid desperation?

It didn't matter. I couldn't afford it. Not now. Lives depended on me thinking straight.

But the image wouldn't fade. Bronze scales. Gold eyes. That growl when the guard hit me.

*Touch what is mine, and I will rip your throat out with my teeth.*

A shiver traced its way down my spine. Not fear. Damn it. Something else entirely. Something hot and confusing and dangerous.

I pressed my palms flat against the cold, gritty floor. *Remember who you are, Cross.* Intel officer.

Survivor. Not some weak-kneed damsel pinning her hopes on a winged alien predator.

But as the night bled towards dawn, as the arena sounds died to an echoing, waiting silence, a traitorous part of me hoped. Against logic. Against survival instinct.

Hoped he'd come.

Hoped he'd fight.

Hoped he'd win.

Hoped that look, that possessive fury, meant something after all.

Sleep finally dragged me under, shallow and restless. Haunted by gold eyes and the bloody promise of dawn.

THE ROOM COULD WAIT. Its stink of desperation and *her* could wait.

Vega's rashness was a clenched fist inside my chest, pulsing heat with every step I took away from that cursed arena. I prowled Ignarath's festering edges instead, the grounds a target under the cold moonlight. Mapping its weaknesses. Cataloging its flaws. The stone itself seemed to drink the light, ancient and thirsty. Iron-banded gates waited, promising violence. Good. Violence I understood.

Night bled away the crowds. Only dregs remained, gamblers rolling dice in the shadows, scarred fighters nursing hatred, the scent of stale blood and desperation thick on the air. Faces cataloged. Weaknesses noted.

Arena patrols. Three of them. Circling in regular

intervals. Arrogant in their routes. One favored his left leg, a distinct limp. Vulnerable. Another wore heavy plate armor, movement sluggish. Advantage. Predictable. Sloppy.

Ignarath confidence was its own kind of rot.

Dust coated my scales when I finally returned to the dilapidated hole we called a room. Sanctuary? It reeked of confinement. I slammed the door, the impact rattling the frame, shaking dust motes down into the gloom.

Relief warred with ... something else. A hollow space where her defiance should have been.

She'd nearly gotten killed. Nearly dragged me down with her. For a glimpse of caged humans? A fool's errand born of misplaced loyalty that almost bought us both a piece of Ignarath dirt.

I paced, restless. My tail lashed the splintered floorboards, a counterpoint to the screaming protest in my useless wing. Physical pain I could manage. Use. It sharpened my focus. But the walls felt too close, pressing in, stealing air. Ignarath's unique stench, old blood, hot metal, piss, decay, clung to everything, somehow made sharper by Vega's lingering scent.

That impossible sweetness cutting through the filth, a brand on my senses.

Sleep? A dead hope. Tomorrow demanded clarity. Strength. Every scrap of tactical cunning I possessed. The twin suns of Volcaryth magnified every weakness. My wing, a liability. My focus ... fractured. My judgment ... poisoned by proximity. Hell.

Clear eyes. Cold calculation. That was the path. Vega's life in the balance. Against the ghosts she chased. Against the thousand jagged edges of this pit. Against the storm surge inside me whenever her scent hit, whenever memory flashed, skin flushing under my touch, pulse hammering against my claws—

Focus. The tournament. Strategy. Bloodsport.

Ignarath's notorious games. Warriors crawled there from every territory, drawn by the promise of glory, coin, or just a cleaner death than their lives offered. Blood fed the sand. I'd tasted it once. Young. Arrogant. I'd paid in pain and shredded pride. I knew the patterns. Knew the unwritten laws etched in scars and bone.

First round: dominance. Posturing and brutality.

Second: ferocity. Unleash the beast.

Third: strategy. Cunning over muscle.

The final rounds? Only the ruthless survived.

And I would be ruthless. Savage. Unrelenting.

For her.

The thought coiled, a viper in my gut. Unwelcome. Persistent. Until I finally slept.

---

Dawn smeared blood-red across Ignarath's jagged spires.

Fitting.

The arena waited to drink its fill.

I strapped on what armor I had, scavenged pieces, scarred leather. Not enough. Never enough in this city. My wing hung useless; a dead weight screaming betrayal. Landbound. Grounded.

Vulnerable.

I bound it up with dark cloth and hoped it would blend in enough with the darker scales of my wing and the hardened leather to not be noticeable.

A queue of killers snaked through the arena's outer ring. Scaled hides in every shade—green, black, rust-red. Crude clubs jostled jeweled hilts. Ritual scars proclaimed allegiance or prowess. Hunger burned in every eye. The same feral need in all of them.

And this was just registration day. Time to show off before the true fights began.

The arena maw gaped, swallowing them. Banners overhead were stiff with forgotten victories. Above, the master's pavilion perched like a vulture's nest, stone and ironwork spitting defiance at the sky. Officials would watch from there. Cold eyes weighing odds.

I fell into line. Murmurs followed. Let them stare. Let them guess. Their judgment was weightless air.

My turn. The scribe didn't look up. Scales faded to sickly yellow, claws stained with ink. Bureaucracy stank the same everywhere.

"Name and territory." Voice flat, bored.

"Zarvash of Scalvaris."

His quill paused mid-stroke. Eyes flicked up then, quick, assessing. My scales. My stance. Lingered on the useless wing. Weakness logged. Let him underestimate.

"Reason for entry?" The standard question, barbed now. Sharpened for me.

"Glory." I kept my voice level, mimicking his boredom. "Challenge. Do I need special dispensation to bleed?"

His tongue darted out, tasting the air. Hunting lies. I met his gaze. Cold stone. Nothing to see.

"Entry fee." Claws scraped parchment.

I tossed the pouch. Tokens scavenged from dead guards. Paltry. He counted, eyes narrowed, then scratched another mark. "Entry four. Report for inspection." He pointed towards a tunnel.

Deeper into the arena I went. Guards watched, spears held ready. Not ceremonial. This was power's dark underbelly. The master's den, carved from volcanic rock, lit by sputtering sconces casting writhing, sickly orange shadows.

A shape loomed behind a slab of stone doubling as a desk. The tournament master. Red-gold scales, thick with ritual scars. Muscle gone soft with age and authority. Power clung to him like heavy incense.

"Scalvaris." He spat it. A curse, not a greeting.

I inclined my head. A lie of respect. He knew it. "Tournament Master."

"Unexpected." Claws drummed slow thunder on the stone. "What brings one such as yourself to our humble arena?"

"Unexpected?" I countered, voice flat. "Your scribe seemed informed."

A smile stretched, all needle-sharp teeth. "Ah. The incident. With your ... property." He settled back, enjoying this. "My guards report you claim an alien creature that was caught trespassing."

"Your guards gossip like hatchlings." He gave no

flicker of reaction to that. "But yes. The human is mine."

"Curious." His gaze probed, peeled back layers. "I've never heard of one from Scalvaris to take slaves. Your lot are so critical of our honored traditions."

"That creature is no person." The lie felt like swallowing sand. "It merely serves a purpose."

He studied me. Looking for cracks. For the truth I hid. He addressed the attendant at the door. "Bring it. I wish to see this ... pet."

Pet. The word ignited fury, a primal roar clawing up my throat.

"Is this standard procedure?" My voice scraped, rough metal on stone.

"For unusual cases?" His smile widened, venomous. "Absolutely. Is there a problem, Scalvaris?"

The trap. Sprung. Refusal meant suspicions confirmed. Compliance risked Vega. Hell.

"No problem." I bit the words off.

The attendant vanished down a side passage. Silence stretched, thick with menace. I stood carved from stone, refusing him the satisfaction of seeing the war raging beneath my scales. If he hurt her ... if they'd harmed her further ...

"Tell me, Zarvash." He leaned forward, heavy

forearms on the desk. Testing. Probing. "Does Darrokar sanction this little adventure?"

Politics. Allegiance. Always. "I answer to the Blade Council and my own judgment. There are no laws against entering this tournament. I've done so before. This year, I plan to win."

"Ambitious." His tongue flicked, tasting the air again. Seeking the flavor of my words.

Before I could form a reply that wasn't a snarl, the attendant returned, dragging Vega behind him.

My vision went red. A tremor started deep in my chest, threatening to erupt. Bound. Hands lashed tightly before her. Dried blood crusted her jaw where some bastard had struck her. Filth smeared her clothes, the stink of the cells clinging to her.

But her eyes. Gods, her eyes still burned. Fierce. Unbroken.

She saw me. Something flickered across her face, relief? Accusation? Gone before I could grasp it, masked by defiant stillness.

I wanted to rip the room apart. Tear the Master's throat out with my bare claws. Snatch her away, cleanse the filth of their touch from her skin. The urge was physical agony, a blade twisting behind my ribs.

Instead: stone. Cold indifference carved onto my face.

"So." The Master rose, circling Vega. Assessing livestock. "This is the pet."

I wanted to flay the word from his tongue. "Yes." Voice flat. I had to keep any emotion out of it. She had to just be a *thing* right now or we were both dead.

He reached out. One claw hovered near the line of her throat. I forced stillness. Forced control.

*Don't react. Don't snarl. Don't give him the satisfaction.*

The rage boiled, scalding, just beneath the surface.

"Spirited." He observed, gaze sliding back to me. "Needs a firmer hand, perhaps."

Vega's eyes met mine. A warning. Understanding. We were balanced on a knife edge.

He circled back, posture radiating expectation. "Prove it."

My jaw tightened. "Prove what?"

He gestured towards Vega, a flick of his wrist. "That you control it."

Control her. The word felt obscene. Alien. Break her spirit for this fat slug's amusement? Bile rose, hot and bitter. But the alternative ... Ignarath justice. For both of us. The performance was necessary. Hating it wouldn't change that.

I stepped towards her. Close. Too close. Close enough to smell the cell-stink, the blood, and beneath it all, irrevocably, her. That sharp sweetness that drove me mad. Her eyes tracked me. Sharp. Wary. Calculating.

"Kneel." The command scraped my throat raw. Felt like tearing scales.

A hesitation. Microscopic. Just enough resistance to be believable, not enough to be fatal defiance. Her gaze locked with mine. *Trust me. Play the part.*

Slowly, she sank. Shoulders tight with tension. Chin lifted, even in submission. Pride bent, not broken. Never broken.

The Master's scales rippled. Amusement? Satisfaction? "Better. But it lacks ... conviction."

He wanted more. A show of absolute dominance. My stomach churned.

Closer still. Looming. Playing the monster they expected. Hating every molecule of air I displaced. I reached out, a feigned strike, a harsh grip on her shoulder, enough force to sell the lie, not enough to inflict true pain—

Then she collapsed.

Sudden, violent. Her forehead slammed against the filth-streaked stone at my feet. A brutal, absolute subjugation that ripped something cold and sharp through my chest.

"Mercy," she choked out, voice carrying in the dead air. Hoarse. Desperate. "Mercy, Master."

Master. Acid to my ears. This fierce, proud woman, groveling. Selling the lie with terrifying conviction. Saving us both.

My turn. I placed one booted foot near her bowed head. A conqueror's stance. "Silence, creature."

She whimpered, and it felt real enough to make me want to hurl, either my breakfast or the Master against the nearest wall.

The Master laughed. "Perhaps you have tamed it after all." He lumbered back to his desk, scratched another mark in his ledger. "You're confirmed for the tournament. Don't be late." He paused, malice gleaming in his small eyes. "But first, the opening feast. Tonight, in the Blood Hall at sunset. All combatants are expected." He paused. "Creatures are welcome."

Creatures. Another trial. My claws dug into my palms, points threatening to break through my scales. "Where is this hall?"

"You'll find it." Dismissive wave. "Now, get your pet cleaned up. It stinks."

The word sparked like flint on steel inside my skull. I hauled Vega to her feet, grip deliberately rough, pulling her, stumbling, towards the tunnel exit. A performance of dominance. Her eyes, when they flickered towards mine, were full of fire.

In the shadows of the corridor, in the Master's view but out of his hearing, I leaned close. A threatening posture.

My whisper hissed against her ear, low, venomous promise.

"We're going to gut them all."

## ZARVASH

THE CITY'S foul breath clung to us both as I dragged Vega back through the labyrinthine alleys of Ignarath. Every shadow seemed to hold eyes, every flicker of movement felt like talons scraping against my scales, probing for weakness, for the slightest crack in my facade.

Her wrists, red and chafed, and the map of bruises blooming across her delicate face were a relentless war drum pounding against the fraying edges of my control with each step.

My grip remained firm on her arm, a calculated pressure, tight enough to sell the brutal ownership demanded by this cursed place yet consciously eased to avoid inflicting more pain. We were a spectacle, a master and his defiant property, and all of Ignarath had eyes. Eyes that reported directly to the Tournament Master, whose leering satisfaction was burned into my memory.

One misstep, one crack in the performance, and our lives were forfeit.

Finally, the warped wood of the guestroom door groaned shut behind us. I slid the heavy, rusted bolt into place, the grating sound echoing in the sudden quiet. I stood motionless, senses straining, listening for the shuffle of footsteps in the corridor, the faintest whisper that might betray surveillance. Only when the silence stretched, thick and undisturbed, did I release her arm, the imprint of her shape lingering on my claws.

"Are you hurt?" The words clawed their way out, rough and grating like shards of obsidian scraping my throat.

Vega rotated her shoulders, a slight wince tightening the bruised corner of her mouth. "Nothing that won't heal."

Her gaze met mine, wary, assessing, but devoid of fear. Not of me, anyway. The crushing weight of our reality pressed down, tangible as the humid air. The Tournament Master's predatory eyes fixed on Vega, the sickening enjoyment he'd taken in her forced submission, the memory sent a fresh surge of black, killing rage through my veins.

"I'm sorry." The apology felt thin, utterly inadequate against the backdrop of her degradation. "For ... all of that."

"Don't." She shook her head, strands of sweat-dampened hair falling across the livid mark on her jaw. "You played your part. We both did what was necessary."

I moved to the narrow window slit, scanning the deserted, refuse-strewn street below. Clear, for now. The water pitcher on the rickety nightstand was half-full, the liquid stale but precious. I poured some onto a scrap of surprisingly clean cloth I found tucked away, then turned back to her.

"Let me." I held up the damp rag, indicating the smear of dried blood clinging to her skin.

She hesitated for a moment. Then, with a small nod, she perched on the edge of the sleeping platform.

I knelt before her, forcing my movements to be slow, deliberate, devoid of the predatory quickness natural to me. The accumulated filth of the cells clung to her, layers of sweat, dried blood, fear, and the unique, pervasive stench of Ignarath's ever-present cruelty. My gut churned at the thought of the humiliations heaped upon her.

Because of me. Because of this damnable, inexplicable bond that tugged at my very bones, demanding I protect her with all I was.

Carefully, I brought the cloth to her face, gently wiping away the dark crust marring the corner of her mouth. Her skin was startlingly warm beneath the damp fabric, soft in a way that still felt profoundly alien against my scaled knuckles. She flinched when the cloth brushed a particularly tender spot near her eye, and I pulled back instantly.

"I'm fine," she insisted. "Keep going."

I resumed but kept my touch light. The cloth came away, stained by blood and dirt. With each slow pass, more of her true face emerged from beneath the grime—pale skin flushed with exertion and lingering adrenaline, the scattering of freckles across the bridge of her nose like distant constellations, the sharp lines of fierceness etched around her mouth and eyes.

"I should have stopped you," I said finally, the words low, tearing against the silence. "When you left. I should have anticipated this."

Her eyes flashed with a spark of defiance. "I am not yours to manage."

"You *are* while we remain trapped in this viper's nest." The words came out harsher than intended, laced with the fury I felt towards her captors, towards myself. I forced my tone to soften. "This city ... Vega, you cannot comprehend the depths of their depravity."

"I think," she countered dryly, "I got a fairly visceral introduction."

The angry red circles around her wrists made my own jaw clench so hard I felt the bones grind. Switching to a clean corner of the cloth, I carefully dabbed at the raw, abraded skin. They had dared to put chains on her.

"Was it worth it?" I asked, keeping my voice low, pitched beneath potential eavesdropping. "The humans?"

Her expression shifted, a fragile flicker of hope breaking through the exhaustion and pain. "Five in the lowest cells, beneath the arena sands. They confirmed it; Kira's sister is alive. But they've moved her, taken her somewhere outside the city walls. And then there were the three that I saw before the guards came. I didn't have much time to talk to them."

"Alive is good. But it changes nothing about our immediate survival."

I moved to rinse the cloth in the remaining water, needing the simple action. When I turned back, water dripping from the rag, she was tugging at the collar of her filthy, sweat-stiffened tunic, grimacing.

"I need to get this off. It reeks of that place."

Before the implications could fully register, before I could form a coherent thought, she pulled the wretched tunic over her head in one swift, decisive motion.

My breath hitched, lodging somewhere high in my throat.

*Look away.*

Honor demanded it. Self-preservation screamed it.

But my eyes refused to obey, locked onto the sight of her, the pale, vulnerable expanse of her skin, the unexpected curve of her breasts bound tightly in some thin, practical wrapping, the brutal, beautiful constellation of purple and blue bruises blooming across her ribs. Wounded. Defiant. Utterly, impossibly alien and yet ...

My hand tightened around the cloth. My mouth was suddenly bone dry. This was madness. Utter, self-destructive insanity. And yet, I moved behind her, drawn by a current stronger than reason, stronger than duty.

Her back was covered in faint, silvery lines of old scars I hadn't noticed before, stark against the fresh, angry bruises left by rough handling, the delicate knobs of her spine leading down to the waistband of her dirt-caked pants. I pressed the cool, damp cloth gently against her skin, starting at the tense line of her shoulders, wiping away the layers of grime in long, slow, careful strokes. My claws, usually weapons, felt clumsy, overly large against her fragile skin.

She let out a sigh, a soft sound of relief that vibrated through the cloth, shivering down my own spine like a physical touch. I continued downward, tracing the elegant line of her backbone, feeling the subtle shift and play of muscle beneath her skin.

That close, her scent threatened to overwhelm my senses, not just the lingering stench of the prison, but something beneath it, that uniquely sweet, almost fiery spice that was intrinsically *her*, cutting through the filth, making my head swim, making my tongue tingle with a phantom taste.

*Mine.*

"Turn," I commanded, my voice rougher than intended, strained.

She obeyed without argument, turning to face me. The thin fabric binding her breasts was now damp, clinging slightly where water trickled down from her neck. I swallowed hard, forcing my focus onto the task.

Clean off the filth. Nothing more.

I started at her collarbone, wiping away sweat and grime, acutely aware of the frantic pulse fluttering beneath the thin skin, a rapid, fragile bird-beat so unlike the slow, heavy thrum of my own heart. I moved lower, my hand hesitating instinctively at the upper edge of her binding.

"It's fine," she murmured, her voice low, intimate despite the circumstance.

Before I could protest or retreat, she reached up, nimble fingers quickly unwinding the stained fabric, letting it fall away to pool at her feet.

The air punched from my lungs. Her breasts were revealed, small, high, perfectly formed, tipped with dusky pink nipples that tightened instantly in the cooler air. A sliver of rational thought screamed *look away, maintain control, this is madness!* But I was transfixed, caught in the gravity of her unexpected vulnerability, her defiant beauty.

"Zarvash." My name, spoken softly on her lips, jolted me back.

I blinked, realizing I'd frozen, rag hovering uselessly in my hand. "Apologies."

I resumed the task, my touch less steady now. I wiped the damp cloth across her sternum, feeling the slight vibration of her heartbeat, then carefully around the gentle curve of each breast. Her skin pebbled beneath the cloth, tiny bumps rising in its wake. A reaction to the cool water. Or something else entirely.

My own scales felt suddenly too hot.

Her breath hitched when my cloth brushed over one tight nipple. The sound shot through me like a Narvix hunting bolt, straight to my cock, awakening something ancient, primal, and ravenously hungry. I forced myself to continue, moving down, mapping the landscape of her ribs, cataloging each bruise with a cold, mounting fury.

When my hand reached the waistband of her trousers, I stopped. This was already miles beyond propriety, beyond the jagged line I was struggling to hold.

"I can manage the rest," she said, taking the cloth from my suddenly numb fingers. Our skin brushed again, the brief contact searing, sending another unwelcome jolt of electric awareness through my veins.

I should have stepped back. Created distance. Reasserted control. But I remained rooted, a statue carved from conflict, as she unfastened the crude ties of her pants and pushed them down her legs, revealing more pale skin marred by scrapes and the darkening shadows of bruises. She wore some thin, practical undergarment beneath, a flimsy barrier that barely concealed the juncture of her thighs.

She began washing her legs, her movements quick, efficient, almost dismissive. But I watched, unable to tear my gaze away, as rivulets of dirty water trickled down her thighs, following the graceful, lean curves of her calves. She was built for speed, for endurance, tightly coiled muscle beneath deceptively soft skin.

A predator in her own right, trapped in a fragile form.

When she finally straightened, the damp cloth falling from her hand to the floor, her eyes locked with mine across the scant feet separating us. Something shifted in the air. It thickened, heavy now with her purified scent, clean skin overlaying that unique, intoxicating fire-spice that had tormented my senses for weeks.

It wasn't merely a smell; it clung to the back of my throat, a tangible taste on my hypersensitive tongue. Madness. Sheer, fucking madness.

"All clean." She made no move to cover herself, standing before me, defiant and vulnerable in the thin, damp undergarment clinging to her skin, her gaze unwavering.

We stood frozen, inches separating us, bound by an invisible, crackling current. Her pulse beat a frantic tattoo, visible at the base of her throat. Mine pounded against my own ribs, a brutal war drum signaling the imminent, catastrophic loss of control.

Duty. Survival. *Her.*

"Vega," I began, the name a rough scrape in my suddenly dry throat, unsure what I intended, an order, a plea, a warning against the inevitable.

She moved. A single, decisive step, closing the final, precarious distance. Or perhaps I surged forward, pulled by forces beyond my command. The distinction vanished as her mouth crashed against mine.

Hells below.

The impact jolted through my entire system, obliterating conscious thought, shattering control. Her lips were impossibly soft, yielding, despite the fierce demand in the kiss.

Instinct, ancient and overwhelming, slammed through me. My arms banded around her. My claws flexed, the tips pressing against her back, requiring conscious, agonizing restraint not to dig deeper, not to break her fragile form.

*Careful. Do not shatter this.*

My tongue, already hyper-aware, was scalded raw, ignited by the intimate contact. It swept into her mouth without permission, a desperate, hungry exploration, mapping every inch of her. This wasn't gentle; it was primal claim, a near-violent, visceral need to consume, to devour.

A low growl tore itself from my chest, deep and uncontrolled. My fangs ached, a deep, burning throb radiating into my jaw, the ancient imperative screaming within me. The urge to bite down, to sink my teeth into the smooth, vulnerable skin of her neck, to *mark* her, was a physical, clawing demand inside my skull.

*Mine.* The word echoed, potent and terrifying.

Her hands gripped my shoulders, fingers digging in surprisingly hard, finding purchase on the thicker scales there, anchoring me, anchoring herself in the storm. She made a sound, a sharp intake of breath swallowed by the kiss, quickly followed by a low, guttural moan dragged from deep in her throat that resonated through my bones, vibrated against my fucking teeth.

My tail, acting on pure, unthinking instinct, coiled around her bare leg until she shivered. The sensitive tip brushed the inside of her thigh, nudging higher, questing, driven by a will of its own.

It found the damp heat gathering at the juncture of her legs, the air thickening further.

She gasped into my mouth, and her hips instinctively, undeniably, bucked against the pressure. Hells. She fucking *ground* against my tail, chasing the friction, speaking a silent, desperate language my body understood perfectly even as my mind recoiled in shock and burning need.

It took Forge blessed strength not to move that tiny barrier of cloth and bury my tail inside of her.

"Zarvash," she breathed against my mouth as I shifted, needing a different angle, needing *more*, needing to ease the agonizing pressure building within me. Her voice was ragged, thick with the same desperate, clawing need that was ripping through the last vestiges of my control.

I tore my mouth from hers, trailing kisses down her sharp jawline, licking greedily at the frantic, vulnerable pulse hammering in her throat. Her scent was overwhelming there—clean skin, female sweat, fear, defiance, and the sharp, intoxicating tang of pure arousal.

It filled my head, drowning rational thought,

drowning everything but the roaring need. My fangs pulsed again, throbbing with the primal urge.

*Need to bite. Need to taste. Need to mark.*

Her hands were suddenly impatient, urgent, fumbling, then yanking brutally at the fastenings of my tunic. The sound of tough leather ties giving way was obscenely loud in the charged quiet. Her cool fingers brushed against my bare scales, sending shockwaves of agonizing pleasure through me. She explored the hard planes of my chest, the sensitive junction where wings met back, her touch both hesitant and demanding.

"We shouldn't," I rasped, the words a blatant lie my body refused to heed, my voice strained, unrecognizable. My cock strained against the unforgiving confines of my trousers, thick, heavy, painfully hard, pressing insistently against the soft curve of her belly through the thin barrier of her undergarment.

"Probably not," she agreed, her voice husky, breathless, before her mouth captured mine again, fiercer this time, obliterating the half-hearted, utterly futile protest.

Her hands slid lower, bolder now, mapping the ridges of my abdomen. Then one hand slipped beneath the waistband of my trousers, calloused fingertips brushing the hypersensitive skin just above my hipbone.

A violent shudder ripped through my entire frame. Control shattered.

Driven by pure instinct, I walked her backward, stumbling, needing unbroken contact, needing to feel every inch of her against me, until the backs of her legs hit the rock of the sleeping platform.

We crashed onto it, a tangle of limbs, desperation, and raw, unleashed need, my weight pinning her beneath me. She arched instantly, hips lifting off the stone, offering herself; a silent, eloquent invitation that scorched through my veins like dragon fire.

*Yes. Now.*

Her hands were suddenly everywhere, mapping the contours of my back, tracing the lines of old battle scars, fingers tangling in the short, coarse spines at the nape of my neck. When her questing fingers brushed the damaged joint at the base of my injured wing, a sharp hiss of pain escaped me despite myself.

She froze instantly. "Sorry," she whispered, pulling back slightly, her eyes wide with concern even now. "I forgot—"

"It does not matter," I cut her off, capturing her mouth again, harder this time, needing to drown the flare of pain, the reminder of weakness, needing to drown everything but *her*, the taste of her, the feel of her beneath me.

She met my kiss with equal, desperate fervor. One slender leg wrapped tightly around my waist, pulling me closer still, grinding her heat against the agonizing hardness straining against my trousers.

The friction, even through the layers of cloth, was torture, pushing me closer to the edge. She rocked against me deliberately now, meeting my involuntary thrusting need, stoking the inferno within.

*Want to bury myself deep inside her. Feel her clench around me. Feel her heat surround me. Now. Need it now.*

Her hand slid down my stomach again, bolder, fingers tracing the thick, rigid length of my erection through the fabric. My hips bucked involuntarily at the direct contact. Need surged, heady and blinding, obliterating everything else. I shifted, trying frantically to align us better, ready to tear away the frustrating barriers between us, ready to finally, finally—

**BLLAAAAARRRR!**

A horn blared from outside, the harsh summons of the Ignarath arena authority slicing through the thick haze of lust like a shard of ice plunged into my heart. The signal. For the damned, cursed feast.

We froze. Locked together, tangled limbs, heaving chests, breath sawing raggedly in the sudden, ringing silence. Reality crashed back, brutal, cold, and utterly unwelcome.

Her eyes, wide and dark, pupils still blown wide with desire, met mine across the scant inches separating us. The flush staining her skin, her swollen, kiss-bruised lips, the near-naked vulnerability of her body sprawled beneath me, it sent another wave of frustrated need crashing through me, nearly sending me over the edge again despite the intrusion.

My own body pulsed with thwarted urgency, the battle to regain even a semblance of composure, a visible tremor in my claws, still pressed against her skin.

"We have to—" I was so reluctant I couldn't finish the sentence, the words scraping my throat raw, tasting like ashes and defeat.

She nodded slowly, the spell violently broken, but the tension remained; thick enough to taste, humming between us like a strained wire.

With a hesitance that felt like tearing living flesh, I pushed myself up, away from her heat, her intoxicating scent, her impossible softness. The loss of contact was immediate, an ache opening up a cold void where her warmth had been pressed so intimately against me only moments before.

She sat up, pushing tangled, sweat-dampened hair from her flushed face. The sight of her, thoroughly kissed, disheveled, lips still bearing the imprint of my mouth, her body a canvas of bruises and raw need, tested my shattered control to its absolute breaking limit.

Turning away sharply before I did something irreparable, something that would doom us both, I forced myself toward the pile of discarded clothing near the door.

"Prepare yourself," I commanded, my voice harsher than intended, strained and rough, brittle with the effort of containing the inferno still raging uncontrolled within me. "The feast will not wait."

THE BLOOD HALL earned its name. Columns made of skulls with eye sockets oozing unnatural red light. The air hit me like a fist. It was rotten with roasting meat, something fermented, and the unmistakable iron tang of fresh blood. My stomach lurched.

Subtle, these Ignarath weren't.

Zarvash's grip tightened around my upper arm as we approached the massive entryway. Not painful, but firm. A reminder.

I was his property. His possession. His prize.

Fuck.

"Ah, the warrior from Scalvaris arrives!" a booming voice cut through the noise. The Tournament Master stepped forward, his bulk somehow more impressive in ceremonial garb—crimson fabric draped over one shoulder, exposing a chest covered in scales and scars glittering with oil.

"Master." Zarvash inclined his head, voice carefully neutral.

"Please," the Tournament Master's smile was all teeth, "such formality is unnecessary tonight. Call me Skorai." He clapped a meaty hand on Zarvash's shoulder. "You honor us with your participation." His eyes slid to me, lingering in a way that made my skin crawl. "And with your ... unusual companion."

"Honor indeed," Zarvash replied, revealing nothing.

Skorai gestured expansively. "The warriors' table awaits. Come."

Zarvash scowled at me. "Make yourself useful." His breath was hot against my ear, claws digging into my arm hard enough to leave pinpricks of blood.

I nodded jerkily. Voice? Gone. Did I trust it if I could manage a squeak? Hell no.

Useful. Right. The word tasted foul. I had to remember who I was to these people.

Just a thing.

Not his ... whatever the hell had happened back in that room. Almost happened. Halfway happened.

My body burned with the memory of it.

My wrists still tingled where he'd touched me,

the ghost of his tongue a phantom brand on my skin. His taste lingered on my lips, and between my legs, a persistent, maddening ache throbbed in time with my pulse. We'd been inches from crossing a line, and then that damned horn blared.

Was I grateful or furious? Hell if I knew.

Zarvash's scales caught the light as he turned away, following Skorai deeper into the Blood Hall. My gaze traced the powerful line of his back, the tight fold of his injured wing, the way his tail swished with barely contained tension.

"Useful," I muttered to myself. "I'll show you fucking useful."

Long tables groaned under platters of meat so rare it still oozed blood. The air, thick, choking. Smoke, roasted flesh, and the pungent musk of too many Drakarn warriors packed into too small a space.

Warriors from every territory huddled around the tables, scales glittering in the torchlight, green, red, black, orange. Trophy belts hung heavy with bones and claws. Weapons gleamed, casually displayed. The atmosphere vibrated with barely leashed violence, predators temporarily agreeing not to tear each other's throats out.

For now.

I moved through the crowd. Head down. Shoulders hunched. Playing submission while my skin crawled with every step. Just another slave. Beneath notice.

My fingers twitched, desperate for my knife. Zarvash hadn't said a word about it when he saw me strap it to my leg. Small mercies from my pretend master. Christ.

The din of Drakarn voices, growls, hisses, and that strange, rumbling laughter that sounded like boulders tumbling down a mountainside, washed over me. My translator caught snatches: boasts about past kills, speculation on tomorrow's matches, crude jokes about who would die first.

I kept moving. Scanning the room. Memorizing exits. Logging guard positions. Intel gathering. That's what I was good at.

Behind the feasting warriors, human slaves scurried like shadows. Heads down, movements quick and efficient, they refilled goblets, replaced empty platters, collected all the discards. Five, just as I'd counted in the cells. There were three more, somewhere. Unless the ones I'd seen right before my capture had been ... dealt with.

I slipped deeper into the hall, angling toward the kitchens where steam billowed through an arched doorway. If I could just get a moment alone with them—

There was a commotion near one of the serving tables. A stocky Ignarath warrior with dull yellow scales had cornered one of the humans, Asif, the quiet one from the cell. The Drakarn loomed over him, one claw wrapped around his thin wrist, yanking him closer.

"Move faster, meat," the Ignarath snarled, forked tongue flickering between sharp teeth. "My cup's been empty too long."

Asif's face was a mask of carefully controlled fear. "Yes, sir," he murmured in clumsy Drarkan, eyes downcast. "Forgive me."

The Ignarath's claw tightened until Asif winced. "Maybe I should teach you—"

"Is there a problem?"

The voice boomed like thunder, deep and commanding. I froze, pressing myself against a stone column, watching as a massive Drakarn materialized beside the Ignarath. He was enormous, even by Drakarn standards, scales a mottled pattern of deep crimson and ash gray. The red flecks scattered across his hide caught the torchlight, gleaming like droplets of fresh blood.

The Ignarath released Asif's wrist, turning. His

posture shifted, aggression bleeding into wariness. "Just disciplining my slave."

"Not yours," the red-scaled giant corrected, voice deceptively mild. "He's tournament property." He leaned closer, and even from my hiding spot, I could see the Ignarath shrink back slightly. "And I don't recall anyone authorizing damage to the arena's assets before the games even begin."

The Ignarath's tongue darted out nervously. "I wasn't—"

"Leave." The single word carried the weight of a death sentence.

For a moment, I thought the Ignarath might challenge him. His claws flexed, wings twitched. But then his gaze dropped, and he slunk away, disappearing into the crowd.

The red giant turned to Asif, who was cradling his wrist, a vivid ring of bruises already forming on his skin. "You're injured."

Not a question, but Asif shook his head anyway. "I'm fine, Master."

The Drakarn studied him for a long moment, then said, quietly, "Don't call me that. My name is Omvar."

Asif's head jerked up in surprise, eyes wide. Mouth opened, closed, then simply nodded.

"Go," Omvar said, gentler now. "Tend to your duties and keep away from that one. He's a mean drunk." He gestured toward where the Ignarath had vanished.

Asif scurried away, casting one last bewildered glance over his shoulder.

Interesting. Very interesting.

I filed the information away—Omvar, a Drakarn who stepped in to help a human, who offered his name instead of a title. Was he actually a good person? Or was I giving him points for the barest fucking minimum? Hard to tell when the bar was set somewhere beneath hell.

Omvar's gaze swept the hall. For a heart-stopping moment, I thought he'd spot me. I pressed deeper into the shadows, holding my breath until he turned and moved toward a table where several other massive warriors sat.

Taking my chance, I slipped into the kitchen area.

The heat hit me like a sledgehammer to the chest. Sweltering. Oppressive. Like breathing through a wet towel soaked in grease. Humans and a few Drakarn slaves worked at a frantic pace, chopping, stirring, hauling trays. No one looked up as I entered, too focused on their tasks.

I spotted Kinsley near the back, her cropped hair damp with sweat as she vigorously stirred something in a massive pot. She was the leader of this pack, the one I needed to get on my side. And her guard was up so high I wasn't sure I'd be able to surmount it. Definitely not tonight. But I had to try.

"I told you I'd be back," I said.

She stiffened and nearly dropped her spoon into the pot. Her head whipped around, eyes wide with panic before recognition set in. "What the hell?" she hissed. "How did you ... If they catch you—"

"I'm with one of the warriors," I said, grabbing a nearby platter of unidentifiable meat and rearranging the meat in piles. "I'm supposed to be his ..." The word stuck in my throat like a chicken bone. "His slave."

Her eyes narrowed. "The Drakarn you mentioned?"

I nodded.

"And he just let you wander off? Bullshit."

*He's my partner, not my master*, I wanted to protest. But I couldn't say those words out loud, not even in English. I wouldn't be that sloppy and risk my cover in this den of Drakarn.

"He's occupied with the Tournament Master." The piles of meat on my tray were looking more and more like mush. "I don't have much time. I need to know more about this place, the tournament, how to get you all out—"

"You can't," she cut me off, voice flat. "No one gets out, not unless they're carried out in pieces for the scavengers." Her gaze drifted to the kitchen entrance, then back to me. "See those three?"

I followed her gaze to where the three humans I'd seen in the cells before my capture were now circulating through the hall. Their clothes were clean now, each had nicely combed hair, and they were moving around like they wanted to be there. One, a woman with long dark hair, was actually smiling as she placed a tray before a Drakarn warrior, who rewarded her with a casual stroke down her arm.

"I saw them before," I said. "They were in a cage on the arena grounds."

"Don't trust them," Kinsley warned, her voice dropping even lower. "They've ... adapted. Found favor. They'd sell any of us out for an extra scrap of meat or a softer place to sleep."

The disgust in her voice was palpable. I studied the three humans more carefully. Their movements were fluid, posture too relaxed. Stockholm syndrome? Or something more calculated? Survival looked different on everyone. Who was I to judge?

"What about Larissa?" I asked. "You said she was taken somewhere outside the city?"

Kinsley's mouth tightened. "Some mining operation, I think. One of the Ignarath officials took a liking to her engineering knowledge." She hesitated. "She fought them at first. Hard. But then ..."

"Then what?"

"Then she stopped. Started cooperating." Kinsley's eyes were haunted. "The last time we saw her, she was different. Quiet. Remote. Like something inside her had just ... switched off."

A cold weight dropped through my gut like a stone. What the fuck had they done to her? Christ. What would I even tell Kira? Found your sister, she's broken inside? My hands were shaking. I curled them into fists.

"What's up with Omvar?" I asked, nodding toward where the massive red Drakarn had taken a seat. "What's his deal?"

Kinsley followed my gaze, expression unreadable. "He's one of the favorites to win. Been champion three years running, they say." She lowered her voice further. "He's ... different from the others.

Doesn't take slaves for himself. Doesn't participate in the ... entertainments they arrange after the feasts."

"Is he trustworthy?"

She barked out a harsh laugh. "None of them are trustworthy. But he's less likely to tear your throat out for looking at him wrong." She glanced toward the entrance again, posture tensing. "You should go. Someone's looking for you."

I followed her gaze and spotted one of Skorai's guards scanning the kitchen, yellow eyes narrowed in suspicion.

"Go," Kinsley urged. "And if you really want to help us? Tell your warrior to win. Then get us the hell out of here."

I slipped away, ducking behind a column just as the guard entered the kitchen area. Heart hammering against my ribs, I made my way back into the main hall, eyes scanning for Zarvash.

I spotted him at the high table, seated among the elite warriors, Skorai at his side. The Tournament Master was leaning close, speaking into Zarvash's ear, a predatory smile stretching his scaled face. Zarvash's expression was a perfect mask of cold indifference, but I could see the tension in his shoulders, the rigid set of his jaw.

Our eyes met across the hall. A silent message,

danger, caution, the reminder of our fragile deception.

I started toward him, weaving through the crowd, when a heavy claw landed on my shoulder. I froze, every muscle tensing for a fight.

"Well, well," a voice drawled into my ear, hot breath against my neck making my skin crawl. "The Scalvaris pet, wandering all alone."

I turned slowly, finding myself face-to-face with one of the guards who'd captured me at the arena. His eyes gleamed like a kid who just found a spider to pull the legs off of. Recognition. Malice. Anticipation.

"My master sent me to fetch refreshments," I said, forcing my voice to sound meek, hating every syllable.

"Did he now?" The guard's claw tightened on my shoulder, talons digging in just enough to sting. "Strange. I could have sworn I saw you talking to the kitchen slaves. In that strange tongue of yours." His other hand came up, tracing a line down my cheek. "Perhaps I should inform the Tournament Master that his guest's pet is misbehaving."

Panic shot through me like an electric current, bright and hot, making my fingers tingle and my mouth go desert dry. If Skorai found out I'd been speaking to the other humans, asking questions ...

I dropped my gaze, forcing myself to lean into his touch instead of recoiling. "Please," I whispered, injecting a tremor into my voice. "My master will punish me severely if he thinks I've displeased him."

The guard's tongue flicked out, tasting the air near my face. "Then I think we can reach an arrangement, pet." His claw slid down my arm, grip loosening slightly. "There's an empty chamber just beyond the kitchens. No one would miss us for a few minutes."

Bile rose in my throat. I swallowed it down, calculating rapidly. I could take him. One quick strike to the throat, my knife between his ribs before he could raise the alarm. But then what? The entire hall would descend on me. Zarvash would be implicated. Cover blown.

I needed another option.

"I ...," I began, but a shadow fell over us, cutting me off.

"There you are."

Zarvash's voice was ice, sharp enough to slice through stone. He materialized beside us, his presence a sudden, overwhelming force. His eyes burned with barely contained fury.

The guard released me instantly, taking a step back. "I was just—"

"Touching what's mine," Zarvash finished, tone casual, deadly. He placed a possessive hand on the back of my neck, claws pricking lightly against my skin. "A mistake you won't make twice, if you value your scales."

The guard's eyes darted between us, calculating, then dropped in submission. "Of course, warrior. My apologies."

Zarvash's grip tightened, steering me away. Once we were out of earshot, he leaned close, breath hot against my ear.

"What were you doing?" he demanded, voice low and tight with anger.

"Reconnaissance," I replied, matching his tone.

"Where did you go? We can't risk discovery."

"You were busy with your new friend," I shot back, unable to keep the edge from my voice. "Besides, I thought I was supposed to be 'useful.'"

His jaw clenched, a muscle ticking visibly beneath his scales. "This isn't a game. One mistake, and we're both dead."

"I know that," I hissed. "But I didn't come all this way just to stand around looking pretty while you make nice with these monsters."

Something flickered in his eyes—frustration, anger, and beneath it all, a flash of that same heat I'd seen back in our room. His gaze dropped to my mouth for a fraction of a second before snapping back up.

"The feast is nearly over," he said, voice rougher now. "Skorai has arranged special ... entertainment to follow. We're expected to attend."

The way he said "entertainment" made my stomach twist. "What kind of entertainment?"

"The kind designed to showcase Ignarath's dominance," he replied grimly. "Fighting pits. Slaves pitted against each other. Or worse."

My blood ran cold. "The humans?"

"Some of them, yes." His expression darkened. "It's considered an honor to have your slave chosen. A chance to display your property's worth."

"And if I'm chosen?" The question slipped out before I could stop it.

Zarvash's eyes met mine, something fierce and protective blazing in their depths. "That won't happen."

"How can you be sure?"

"Because," he said, voice dropping to a growl that vibrated through my bones, "I've made it very clear what happens to anyone who touches what's mine."

There it was again. That word. Mine. It should have infuriated me. Instead, it sent a treacherous shiver down my spine, a warm curl of something I refused to name unfurling in my belly.

Damn it.

A horn blared, signaling the end of the feast. Warriors began to rise from their tables, moving toward an archway at the far end of the hall. Guards herded the human slaves in the same direction.

"Stay close," Zarvash murmured, his hand sliding from my neck to my lower back, guiding me forward. "And whatever happens next, remember why we're here."

I nodded, steeling myself as we followed the crowd. The archway led to a smaller chamber, ringed with stone benches that descended toward a central pit. The floor of the pit was sand, dark, rust-colored sand that I realized with a sickening lurch was stained with old blood.

Warriors jostled for the best seats, their excitement a heady force in the air. Zarvash led me to a spot near the top, positioning himself so that his body partially shielded me from view.

Skorai appeared at the edge of the pit, arms raised for silence. The crowd quieted, anticipation humming through the chamber.

"Warriors of Volcaryth!" Skorai's voice boomed. "Tonight, we offer you a taste of tomorrow's glory. A glimpse of the blood that will flow in our sacred arena!"

A roar of approval shook the chamber. Beside me, Zarvash remained perfectly still, expression carved from stone.

"First, a demonstration of strength!" Skorai continued. "Two slaves, chosen for their spirit. Only one will leave."

A murmur rippled through the crowd as two humans were shoved into the arena—a man I didn't recognize and Nat, the lean, angular woman from the cells. They were each handed crude weapons, the man a short, dull blade, Nat a wooden staff with a metal tip.

"Fight!" Skorai commanded.

The man lunged immediately, desperation making him reckless. Nat sidestepped, bringing the staff around in a swift arc that caught him in the ribs. He staggered but didn't fall.

The crowd jeered, hungry for blood.

The fight below was brutal, neither combatant holding back. Survival instinct had overridden any sense of camaraderie. Nat was quicker, more precise, but the man had strength and desperation on his side.

A particularly vicious blow from his blade opened a gash on Nat's arm. She stumbled, nearly losing her grip on the staff. The crowd roared its approval.

I couldn't watch. Couldn't stand by while humans were forced to slaughter each other for Drakarn entertainment. My fingers found the hilt of my hidden knife, mind racing through scenarios—create a distraction, cause a panic, anything to stop this barbaric display.

Zarvash's hand closed over mine, stopping me. "Don't," he warned, voice barely audible. "You can't save them. Not like this."

"I can't just—"

"You must," he insisted. "For now."

Below, the fight had turned. Nat, bleeding but unbroken, executed a perfect sweep with her staff, knocking the man off his feet. Before he could rise, she was on him, the metal tip of her staff pressed against his throat.

The chamber fell silent, all eyes on Skorai.

The Tournament Master studied the tableau for a moment, then raised his hand, thumb extended. Slowly, deliberately, he turned it downward.

Death. He was ordering her to kill a fellow human.

Nat's face was a mask of conflict, horror, revulsion, the desperate will to survive. Her hands trembled on the staff.

"Do it," the man beneath her whispered, loud enough for those closest to hear. "Better you than them."

A tear slid down Nat's cheek. Then, with a swift, decisive move, she drove the staff home.

The crowd erupted in cheers. Nat stood, blood-spattered and hollow-eyed, as guards dragged the man's body away.

My stomach heaved. I swallowed hard, tasting bile.

"Worthy entertainment!" Skorai proclaimed. "Now, for our main display—a true test of mastery!"

At his signal, a side door opened, and three Drakarn warriors entered the pit, each leading a human on a chain. I recognized them as the three I'd seen earlier, the ones Kinsley had warned me about. The collaborators.

"These slaves have pleased their masters well," Skorai announced. "Tonight, they will demonstrate their loyalty."

What followed turned my stomach. The humans

performed like trained animals, executing combat moves on command, demonstrating their "training" with an eagerness that couldn't be entirely feigned. The crowd alternately cheered and mocked, placing bets on which human would perform best.

Throughout it all, Zarvash remained silent beside me, his body radiating tension. When one of the Drakarn masters ordered his female slave to kneel before him in a gesture of absolute submission, then rewarded her with a possessive stroke down her spine, I felt Zarvash's entire frame go rigid.

"Is this what you expected?" I murmured, unable to keep the bitterness from my voice.

"Worse," he replied, his eyes never leaving the display below. "This is ... degradation. Even by Ignarath standards."

When the "demonstration" finally ended, Skorai returned to the center of the pit. "Tomorrow, warriors, you will spill your blood for glory! Tonight, we honor those who will fight!" He gestured expansively. "The pleasure dens await! Enjoy all that Ignarath has to offer!"

The crowd began to disperse, warriors heading back to the main hall or toward other doorways that presumably led to the "pleasure dens" Skorai had mentioned. I didn't want to think about what happened there.

We made our way through the crowd, Zarvash's hand firmly on my lower back, guiding me toward the exit. We'd nearly reached it when Skorai materialized before us, blocking our path.

"Leaving so soon, Scalvaris?" the Tournament Master inquired, his smile not reaching his eyes. "The night is young."

"I must rest before tomorrow's combat," Zarvash replied, tone neutral but cold.

Skorai's gaze made me want to curl up and die. "And your pet? Perhaps she would enjoy some ... companionship while you prepare."

Zarvash's hand tightened on my back, his claws pressing into my skin through the thin fabric of my tunic. "She stays with me."

"Most warriors are eager to share their prizes. Or at least display them," Skorai remarked, his tongue flicking out to taste the air between us.

"I'm not most warriors." Zarvash's voice had dropped to a dangerous rumble.

For a tense moment, they stared at each other, an unspoken challenge hanging in the air. Then Skorai stepped aside, that cold smile still fixed on his face.

"Of course. Rest well, Scalvaris. You will need it."

SAND CLUNG to my scales from training, gritty, persistent, invasive. I brushed it away for the third time. Tension coiled through my muscles. Dawn had long broken, but in the arena? Time lost meaning. Only the distant crowd's roar marked its passage. Each collective gasp was another warrior's triumph.

Or demise.

My turn approached. Knowledge sat like molten stone in my gut.

"Harkon hasn't lost a match in the preliminary rounds for three tournaments," Vega said, voice low. Pacing. Always pacing. The cramped champion's preparation chamber barely contained her restless energy. "But he's slow to start. It takes him time to find his rhythm."

I watched her—the shadows beneath her eyes

telling their own story. Neither of us had slept. The memory of her body beneath mine, the taste of her mouth, the desperate heat between us, it had haunted the dark hours, even as she'd hidden away in that damned little corner of the room.

"Is that so?" I adjusted the leather binding my damaged wing until it was tight enough to make me gasp. Painful. Necessary. "And where did this tactical assessment come from?"

Her pacing stopped. Eyes flashed—that stubborn defiance. "I listen. I watch." A simple declaration. "It's what I do." Her haze flicked to my bound wing. "That binding won't do much if he gets a direct hit."

"Then I won't give him the opportunity." I wasn't worried about Harkon. I'd been little more than a boy when I tried myself on these sands all those years ago. Today I was a blooded warrior.

Her mouth tightened, worry disguising irritation. "I spoke with the humans last night. They've been forced to attend every tournament since they were captured. And Ignarath loves its fucking tournaments. They say Harkon fights like he's half-asleep until first blood, his opponent's or his own. Then he becomes ..." she searched for the word, "feral."

"Did you learn anything else while risking our cover?"

Irritation crossed her face. "The humans are kept in three separate locations. The ones they locked me with are 'common slaves' as they call them." Disgust colored the words. "The three collaborators are usually housed in slightly better conditions near the pleasure dens. And the skilled ones like Larissa are kept at specialized camps outside the city."

"How far outside?"

"No clue."

I stood and stretched muscles wound too tight. The chamber was suffocating, barely large enough for one warrior, let alone two beings caught up in each other's gravity. Vega's presence filled the remaining space. Her scent mingled with arena dust. The tang of oil I'd used on my scales. The faint hint of old blood permeated everything in this cursed place.

"I tried to speak with Harkon at the feast," I said, checking my blade's edge one final time. Steel caught torchlight. "He didn't say a word to anyone. Didn't touch food or drink."

"Maybe he was meditating on all the ways he plans to dismember you," Vega offered with false brightness.

My eyes narrowed. "Your optimism is inspiring."

A hint of a smile tugged at her lips. She

suppressed it quickly. "I'm just being realistic. You're going into this with a significant disadvantage." Her gaze lingered on my wing. Too long. Too knowing.

"It's not a fight to the death," I reminded her. Cold comfort. Preliminary rounds rarely ended in death, at least officially. But "accidents" happened. Especially when Skorai took interest in the outcome.

"Unless the Tournament Master decides otherwise," Vega echoed my thoughts with unsettling precision. "He doesn't strike me as the type to let rules get in the way of a good spectacle."

She was right. The Tournament Master's eyes had followed us too closely at the feast. He sensed something—perhaps not the truth, but enough to make him a danger to us.

"I could make it look like a fight," I said, words tasting like ash, "then yield. One loss and I'm out of the tournament."

Vega's eyebrows shot up. "You'd throw the match? Is that what you want?"

No.

The very suggestion made something primal surge against my ribcage, roaring in rebellion. I was a warrior of Scalvaris. We did not yield. Did not surrender. But neither did we typically participate in

Ignarath bloodsport for the entertainment of enemies.

"It would simplify matters," I said, not meeting her gaze.

"Would it, though?" She stepped closer. Her body heat washed over me, and I had to fight back the urge to reach out to her. I couldn't afford the distraction before the fight. "You think Skorai will just let us walk out of here if you lose?" She shook her head. "Besides, I can work while you're fighting. Everyone will be distracted by the tournament."

Her logic was sound, but it wasn't just strategy driving her. I could see it, the fierce light in her eyes. She wouldn't abandon the humans she'd found. Not when they were so close.

"I can't protect you while I'm in the arena." The admission burned. I hated the vulnerability.

"I don't need protection," she scoffed. "I need time. Keep them focused on you." A pause, then softer, "Just don't get yourself killed. I'd be very annoyed."

The understatement almost made me laugh. "I'll try to spare you the inconvenience."

A horn blared from somewhere above, signaling the next match. My match.

Vega's expression shifted. Something vulnerable

flickering across her face, gone before in fully formed. She stepped closer until her breath brushed against my scales.

"Don't die," she repeated, and then, swift, unexpected, she rose and pressed her lips against mine.

Brief contact. Fleeting heat. But it sent lightning through my system. Stone struck by storm. By the time my brain registered, she pulled away.

"For luck," she murmured. Not meeting my gaze.

Before I could respond, before I could process the storm unleashed, the chamber door swung open. A guard stood in the entrance and beckoned.

"Time, Scalvaris," he grunted. "The sands await."

I turned to follow but paused at the threshold and looked back at Vega. She stood in the center of the room, arms crossed tightly. Suddenly small and fragile in the vast darkness. An illusion. She was anything but fragile.

"Stay out of trouble," I said.

Her lips curved. That crooked, cynical smile becoming strangely familiar. "Of course, Master." The words were for the guard, but that smile was all for me.

I'd never believed anything less.

The guard led me down a long, torch-lit corridor

that sloped upward. With each step, the crowd's roar grew louder, a thunderous wave of bloodlust pressing against my scales.

There was an iron gate at the end of the corridor. Beyond—the arena proper. Slivers of blinding sunlight cut through the bars. And echoing all around was the stamp and shuffle of thousands awaiting violence.

The currency of entertainment in Ignarath.

"Your opponent is already in position," the guard informed me in a bored tone. He'd witnessed this ritual countless times. "Remember the rules. Yield or unconsciousness only. Kill without permission, and the Master will be angry."

The gate groaned open, metal scraping stone. It sounded like claws on bone. Like death's own door yielding. Blinding light flooded in. With it, the full force of arena noise.

I stepped forward and squinted against the glare of twin suns overhead. The sand beneath my feet was hot, treacherous. Deliberately so. Good footing meant survival. Bad footing meant death. A simple way to even the odds.

The arena was a massive oval with tiered seating made of rickety wood. Thousands of Ignarath filled those seats, scales glinting in harsh sunlight, wings half-spread to catch a meager breeze. Above it all, in a shaded pavilion draped with crimson, sat Skorai and the officials. Vultures awaiting carnage.

And across the sand, my opponent waited.

Harkon was massive even by Drakarn standards. His scales were a mottled gray like weathered stone. His weapon was a hybrid between shovel and battle-axe, the blade crusted with what looked suspiciously like dried blood.

Old victories. Ancient suffering.

He stood motionless. Eyes fixed on me, expression hidden behind a partial mask of hammered metal covering the lower part of his face. It was an unsettling effect. Faceless. Emotionless.

I drew my blade. It wasn't the familiar weight of my battle sword. That had fallen on the field outside of Scalvaris before Vega and I were taken. But I'd taken this one from the champion's armory, and it was adequate. The weight settled into my palm, an extension of my arm, of my will. The crowd's roar intensified. They were hungry for the violence to begin. For blood to feed the sand.

Skorai rose and spread his arms wide. Silence fell.

The Master knew how to control a crowd.

"People of Ignarath!" His voice carried effortlessly. "Today we witness skill against strength, strategy against savagery!" A pause for effect. "Zarvash of Scalvaris faces Harkon of the Eastern Territories!"

Cheers erupted, drowning whatever else he said. Meaningless formalities. This was not about words; it was about bloodshed.

Harkon was still motionless. Unnatural in his stillness. Meditative, almost. I circled slowly, testing the sand. My injured wing was bound tight against my back, an unending reminder of my vulnerability. I couldn't let him touch it.

The horn blared the combat signal. My muscles coiled, ready for the strike.

Nothing.

Harkon remained motionless, his massive weapon held loosely. Eyes tracked my movement with detached interest. A predator deciding whether its prey was worth pursuit.

Vega's words echoed: *It takes him time to find his rhythm ...*

I could use that. Press the advantage early, before his full engagement. But rushing against an opponent his size? Foolish. Patience. Let him make the first mistake.

We circled. The crowd's enthusiasm was waning

as seconds stretched into minutes. No action. Boos rippled through the stands. Ignarath audiences—not known for patience. Or restraint.

"Fight, cowards!" someone shouted from the upper tiers. Others joined. Discontent spread like wildfire.

Harkon's eyes narrowed slightly, a reaction. Pressure mounting. Good.

I feinted. A quick step forward followed by immediate retreat. Testing. Probing. His response was minimal, a slight shift in his stance. Nothing more. But telling. He waited for commitment. For a real attack he could counter with that massive weapon.

I wouldn't oblige.

I continued circling instead. Forcing him to adjust. To follow my movement. Each step in the hot sand cost more energy. Each moment under the suns drained stamina.

Let him feel it first. Let exhaustion be my ally.

A flash of movement in the stands caught my attention—something out of place and causing trouble. I resisted a direct look, but it didn't matter.

The momentary distraction cost me. Harkon lunged, his massive weapon arcing through air with surprising speed. I twisted aside and barely avoided the blade as it sliced through space where my head had been a heartbeat earlier.

The crowd roared in approval. First blood nearly drawn.

I countered. Blade flashing, scoring a glancing blow against his forearm. Not deep enough to stop him, but deep enough to sting. His eyes widened, something shifting behind them, awareness.

Awakening.

He came again. Movements no longer sluggish but precise. The shovel-axe whistled through the air, forcing me to dance backward. Sand shifted treacherously beneath our feet. Again and again, he pressed. Each swing more controlled than last. Finding his rhythm just as Vega warned.

I deflected. Dodged. Waited for openings. They existed, small windows as he recovered from each massive swing. Exploiting them meant getting dangerously close to the lethal edge.

And then I stumbled, my injured wing throwing off my balance for a critical fraction of a second. Harkon saw it. Adjusted and brought his weapon sweeping low across the sand. I leaped. Not high enough. The edge caught my leg, opening a shallow gash along my calf.

Blood welled and dripped.

That sent the crowd into a frenzy of cheers and fresh bets. Harkon's eyes gleamed with new intensity. Just as described. He was awake now. A predator fully engaged.

Pain lanced up my leg. I pushed it aside. Harkon moved differently now. More fluidly. Hesitation was gone from his attacks. His weapon was an extension of his body. Each swing flowed seamlessly into the next, forcing an increasingly desperate defense.

I needed to change the pattern, to break his momentum.

The next time he swung, I stepped into the attack. His eyes widened in surprise. I was inside his guard. Too close for his weapon to be effective. My blade flashed, opening a gash across chest—shallow but definitive.

Blood for blood.

He staggered back, momentarily thrown by the unexpected counter. I pressed the advantage, blade dancing in precise, economical arcs. Forcing defense rather than attack. Each strike calculated for maximum damage. I targeted vulnerable points: inside his elbow, the junction of neck and shoulder, wrist tendons.

But Harkon wasn't finished. He recovered quickly, readjusting his grip on his weapon. He used the handle to block strikes while keeping his blade in constant, threatening motion. We fell into a deadly rhythm.

Attack and counter. Thrust and parry. Neither gaining clear advantage.

Crowd noise faded to a distant roar as my focus narrowed to the immediate: my next heartbeat, next breath, next exchange. Time stretched and compressed. Measured only in burning muscles and the sting of fresh wounds.

A vicious swing forced me to dive and roll across burning sand. I came up crouching, my scales coated in sand. Just in time to see Harkon charging, weapon raised high for an ending blow.

No time to dodge. No space to retreat.

I braced. Blade angled upward in a desperate gambit. His momentum carried him forward in an unstoppable avalanche of Drakarn fury. Impact jarred through our arms as our weapons connected. Force drove him backward, our feet sliding in treacherous sand.

We were locked together for a breathless moment, his greater weight bearing down. I forced my blade closer and closer to his throat as his eyes burned into mine. Searching for weakness. Fear.

He found neither.

With a desperate surge of strength, I twisted and redirected his force rather than opposing directly. He stumbled forward, overbalanced. Vulnerable for a critical moment.

My blade found a gap in the armor behind his knee. Cut deep and severed tendons.

Harkon roared, a bellow of pain and rage echoing off the arena walls as he collapsed. He still clutched his weapon in his claws. But the damage was done. He couldn't stand. Couldn't fight.

The crowd fell silent.

I circled to face him, my blade steady. Waiting. Protocol demanded he yield. Honor required it, even in the savagery of the pit.

"Yield," I said, my voice carrying in the sudden quiet.

Harkon's eyes met mine. Rage gave way to something else—resignation, perhaps. Or respect. Slowly, deliberately, he tossed his weapon in the sand before him in formal surrender.

I glanced at Skorai's pavilion, waiting for judgment. The Tournament Master stood, face impassive. He extended his hand horizontally and accepted Harkon's yield.

No death today.

My leg throbbed, blood seeping into the sand.

Smaller cuts stung across my arms and torso. My damaged wing ached fiercely from exertion.

But I had won. Survived. Advanced.

Guards appeared to help Harkon from the arena. As they passed, he paused and met my eyes. Slowly, he inclined head in a warrior's acknowledgment. I returned the gesture.

Respect for respect.

The crowd was already turning its attention to the next bout. The next spectacle. I limped toward the exit gate. Adrenaline ebbed, leaving exhaustion.

This fight had cost me. And they would only get harder from there.

ALONE. Finally.

The echo of violence still buzzed in my blood. Every time I watched Zarvash take a hit, I clenched around a cold spike of terror; every time his claws raked or he landed a blow, heat surged, primal and fierce, beneath my sternum. I was exhausted and wired, shaking with the relief of it all.

I dragged myself to the battered ceramic basin beside the rickety window, the water inside splashing around my shaking hands. The rag was almost clean and rough enough to score skin. Zarvash was in the middle of the room, broad back turned to me.

Bronze scales dulled under a crust of arena sand were scored by fresh blood. The air between us was thick: copper tang, scorched iron, the wild ozone scent that was all him.

"Sit." It should have sounded gentle, but it was scraped bare with hunger and fatigue. I nodded at the sleeping platform; there was nowhere else for him to go.

He hesitated, that proud line of his jaw tightening, chin lifting a fraction as if deciding whether to take orders from a fragile human. Then, movement. Minimal, efficient. He lowered himself until I imagined the stone groaning beneath his weight.

"Your leg," I said, knees already hitting the floor. But this wasn't about submission. Not in there, with no prying eyes.

The wound streaking his calf was an angry gash, long and oozing, sand and blood glittering in the gloom. My fingers hovered before the first touch, knowing it would hurt. He didn't flinch. He just watched with those disconcerting, gold eyes. Despite the stillness, he seemed coiled, restraint wound tight enough to snap.

I pressed the rag to his skin. My own heart thudded faster, stupidly, irrationally, as if blood and dust and brutal beauty were a new form of oxygen.

"You fought—" I swallowed the word "well"; it was too small for what he'd done in the pit. "You're still here."

"Harkon was tenacious," he ground out.

"But you were smarter." My voice was too high, the last dregs of worry not quite faded. "That feint with the damaged wing? Inspired."

A huff of breath, almost a snort, brushed the hair at my temple as I leaned in, dabbing at a cut above muscle so thick I could barely dent it. "Not a feint," he muttered.

I kept working, rag turning the water a muddied red-brown. I tried for detachment, but the scent of him invaded my senses, dizzying, too much. My fingers, traitorous, lingered an impossibly long beat tracing the wound on his forearm. Testing the edge of hurt, or perhaps, invitation.

"Did you find anything?" he asked, eyes unblinking, unreadable.

"They move the humans between holding cells during the main events. There's a window of stupidity, and the guards get distracted by the fights."

"We'll keep that in mind," was his only response.

At last, I'd cleaned what I could. I was no medic, but I was pretty sure the cuts were superficial. "Turn," I said, voice steadier than my hands. "Your wing."

"It's functional," he bit out.

"Is it?" If that wing didn't heal, we'd be trying our luck out of there on foot, and I didn't like our odds.

He resisted. Pride was not decorative with Zarvash; it was carved deep into his bones. But then there was another sound, somewhere between a grunt and the click of a tongue. He presented the wounded wing, the gesture a surrender and a dare.

I unwound the binding carefully. The membrane underneath was ugly, swollen, inflamed, scales an oil-slick sheen that was worryingly dark. My own shoulder tingled in sympathy, imagining old injuries lit by pain.

"God, Zarvash." My touch skimmed along the edge, feather-light, afraid of shattering more than just pride. "Does ... this ...?" I pressed, just shy of the most discolored joint.

Air hissed between his teeth. "Karys's flaming breath, yes."

I jerked back, palm stinging from the memory. "You can't keep ignoring this." Soft, but the threat of fury was there, coiled inside helplessness. "I think this is infected. We need to find a healer. If you want to survive—"

"I am aware." He growled it, but softer, pain, not anger, vibrating through each word. "I do not require a human to tally my failures."

I could have snapped, spat back an arsenal of barbed retorts. Instead, the exhaustion won out.

"Fine. Lose it. Die spectacularly. Let someone else mop up your mess." I rose, and water sloshed and splattered my boots.

He caught my wrist, lightning fast. Not bruising, just undeniable. Those claws thrummed under my pulse, a reminder of what he could be. What he chose not to be.

"I did not mean ..." His jaw jumped, a muscle ticking. Eyes molten gold and troubled. "Weakness. It is not ... permitted. Here." A confession forced through teeth. The kind of thing I'd seen break men and monsters alike.

Something twisted in me. Anger gone, replaced by longing or dread, I couldn't tell them apart anymore. "We're both in the fire."

I went back to his wing, wrapping it in fresh strips torn from my own faded tunic, soft, worn, heavy with the ghost of soap and sweat. It was the most I could give. When I finished, silence thickened, hot, expectant, like the space before lightning.

"Try not to lose it tomorrow," I managed, attempting a smirk.

A dry, half-chuckle rattled his chest, the sound ghostly after so much violence. "Your concern is noted."

"Self-preservation. I'm not breaking out without

my seven-foot death machine." The joke hurt, familiar and barbed.

He turned. The eyes that found me were shadowed, but the gold sparked, hunger, longing, need, or simply the certainty that neither of us were immune. "Is that all I am, Vega? Death?"

The question landed between us like a dropped weapon, fatal, if you hesitated too long. My logic supplied all the right reasons to turn away, but it was already too late. My body was drawn, hooked on the current of him, and I didn't want to swim free.

"What else," I whispered, closer now, "would you be to me?"

He moved, a predator's grace in every inch. The heat of his body spilled into mine, breath hot with the promise of fire. Spice and metal. Lightning in a bottle.

"You know," he rumbled. No room for doubt in his tone.

My heart battered my ribs like a hawk on volcanic updrafts. My reflexes screamed *turn back, abort, retreat.* I shut them up with a single breath, closing the gap.

His mouth on mine was nothing like the hunger I'd imagined, sharp and bruising. No, this was a question, a prayer. Lips scorching-soft, sliding over mine, salt and copper and dark honey, tasting of blood and iron and everything I didn't have a name for. A tremor licked through me, equal parts terror and awe.

He pulled back, only enough for his forehead to rest against mine, the air charged and wild. His claws cupped the back of my neck, impossibly gentle, somehow. "Do you want me to stop?"

The word hovered at the back of my throat. Stop. This is madness. This is—

"No," I breathed instead. Not surrender. Command.

Something in him loosened. Before I could regret it, his mouth was back on mine, demand rising with the kiss. More pressure, more hunger: tongue tracing, requesting, tasting. I parted, heat and want dissolving caution, and he slid inside, a question that answered itself.

The world shrank to the fire burning along that line, mouth to mouth, chest to chest, pain to want.

I felt a rumble begin deep in his chest before it was heard. He shifted, pulling me up and over, until I straddled his lap. His hands, big enough to crush me, settled at my hips—cool scales losing their chill with each heartbeat. His chest, all hard planes and ancient scars, pressed to mine. My hands moved by instinct to his shoulders—mapping each patch of scale, cataloguing every uneven seam and battle worn ridge.

"*Veshari*," he ground out against my mouth, a word, a vow, a wound refusing to close. "I have wanted—"

"Shh." I pressed my forehead to his. "No words. Just—"

He understood me perfectly.

He shifted, gentle, inhuman strength turning me, lowering my body until the stone of the sleeping platform met my spine and his weight caged me in. My battered dignity should have screamed protest, but his weight felt like armor. His hands skimmed my sides, scaled, calloused, stopping at the hem of my tunic. He waited, asking permission in the tilt of his head.

My nod was shaky but real. He peeled the cloth away, every inch of drag broadcasting need, the thrill of exposure. When at last the fabric pooled at my arms and neck, his breath caught on a barely concealed invocation.

"You are ...," he managed, then faltered. His hands hovered as if he was afraid to dishonor, to presume.

"Different," I finished for him, a shuddering laugh, half-mortified, half-exhilarated.

"Beautiful." It landed like a hammer against the anvil of my fear. His mouth pressed to the hollow of my throat, tongue drawing a molten line to my collarbone, searing pleasure in its wake as he journeyed even lower.

His tongue, hotter than any human's, shockingly agile, circled one nipple, the sensation a jolt straight between my legs. My gasp was needy, desperate, shame and want tangled together.

This wasn't supposed to happen. Not with a Drakarn. Not with *him*. But nothing could make me stop. Not now.

Fumbling fingers found his tunic, wrestling clumsily with unfamiliar fastenings. He helped, until he was bare to the waist, scars crisscrossed his chest, glinting silver in the room's half-light. I traced one along his ribs, felt him shiver at the featherlight touch.

I wanted to remember this, every mark, every story written in his flesh. His hands found the waistband of my pants, claws large, careful. "May I?" he asked, voice softer than the cell deserved.

I nodded, lifting my hips. The fabric scraped away inch by inch, dragging heat across skin. I swallowed, acutely aware of my thin underwear, of skin prickling where his gaze followed fabric's retreat.

He was all slow burn, eyes feasting on the awkward expanse of pale human limb, the wild contrast of hips and breasts and shivering belly. "I have imagined, *veshari*," he said, voice sharpened by awe and need. "But reality—Karys's flame."

There was that word again. I was beginning to know what it meant when a Drakarn called you something special, but I couldn't let myself think about that right now.

"Your turn," I said.

He hesitated, his first true show of uncertainty. "My form is not—" he started.

"I want to see you."

Dark amusement lurked behind his hunger. He slid his trousers down, unhurried, letting each inch of scale and muscle appear in the dim light. When at last he stood bare, I forgot language for a long second.

His cock emerged from a nest of dark red scales at the base, thick, too thick, impossibly so, glistening with translucent slick. Veins knotted under the surface, a tangle of vermillion and gray. The head ... God. A flexible, ridged lip curled protectively over the glans, a living, quivering fringe that gleamed wetly. It wasn't just a difference of shape; it was a new discipline—a lesson in evolutionary innovation.

"You stare." There, a heartbeat of vulnerability, splintered through the rough growl.

"Just ... um, wow," I wheezed. "Alien cock, one. Vega, zero."

A rare, genuine laugh burst out of him. He lowered himself back into reach, letting me trail my curious, shaking hand along the base, where the scales grew softer, heat pouring off him in savage waves. Higher—the flesh smoothed to living velvet, rigid beneath my thumb, that strange, suckling ridge at the tip curling like a sentient thing.

His hiss vibrated through the stone and up my arm, a threat or a warning, I wasn't sure. "Almost too much."

I worked my hand over his length, learning his architecture through touch—slick heat, impossible thickness, pulsing, quivering. The ridge at the tip curled against my thumb, living, questing. He bucked, claws gouging fresh canyons in the rock, restraint nearly atomized.

God, what would it feel like to have that thing in me?

"Feels good?" I tested, daring, and the sound he made was seismic, a deep, demonic groan, full of things older than words.

His tail, until now coiled, whipped violently

against the bed. I might have been scared if it didn't make me shiver with want. I'd heard how Drakarn could use their tails. And right then, curiosity was killing me.

Bolder, I stroked him, finding a rhythm that felt obscene and perfect, wonder and power sparking through my arm. There was a heady pleasure in watching him shake, the baddest thing in the pit undone by the smallest of touches.

His hand closed around my wrist, gentle, but ironclad. *"Veshari."* Voice cracking—edge of prayer and warning. "Stop now, or—" The rest was carved in fire between us.

I could have pushed, could have made him unravel, but his need was thick as honey in the air.

Then he moved, muscles rolling with the promise of violence, down my body, his heat blistering where thighs pressed on either side of my waist. I expected fingers. Instead, it was the tip of his tail, scaled, prehensile, impossibly sensitive, that ghosted over my thigh, drawing spiral patterns, promise and threat entwined.

He slid the fabric down. My body jolted when his hands bracketed my hips, forcing my thighs apart. His nostrils flared, a wisp of breath against my over-heated skin. "Your scent, *veshari*, it is wildfire."

I should have felt exposed, split open in the hard light of alien attention. Instead, want overrode fear. His tail's tip found the seam of my body, circling, teasing, mapping. Sensitive skin screamed under the onslaught, nerves lighting up like a lightning storm.

When he first touched my center—a careful, swirling pressure—the sound I made was raw, uncontrolled, somewhere between prayer and profanity. My hips jerked, answered by his tail teasing near my thigh.

He watched me, obsessively cataloguing every gasp and tremor. His tail slipped higher, sliding slickness where need bloomed bright. He ringed me, teasing, coaxing, until I was shaking under the effort not to shatter.

"More," I demanded. Who was I kidding? I was begging.

He obliged, finding a rhythm that matched my racing pulse, methodical, devastating. One calloused thumb flicked a nipple, doubling the neural overload. There was no room for shame.

The pressure coiled, a storm gathering at the root of my body, wound tighter and tighter with each lap of his tail. I was a live wire waiting for the strike.

"Zarvash—" I collapsed his name into a shudder, because language was leaving me. "I'm—"

He pressed close, voice a thunderhead against my skin. A command and a promise. "Let me see you burn."

That was all it took. The world fractured. Nerve endings detonated, a white-hot solar flare, pleasure unspooling in a silent scream that left me arched and shaking and utterly unmoored. His tail didn't stop; he was wringing me through crest and aftershock, savoring every pulse and tremor as if it were the only thing that mattered.

At last, I collapsed back, a slick mess of sweat and don't-care-anymore, the world spinning down to the size of his eyes, satisfied, intense, unbearably smug.

"Smug beast," I rasped, not quite coherent.

He flexed his hands, golden gaze burning. "Your pleasure is tribute enough."

I reached down, finding him still impossibly hard, hot and slick, impossibly needy. "Let me," I whispered, hoarse with want.

His hand caught my wrist. "*Veshari.*" There was caution in the gravel of his voice. "Are you certain? This is not demanded of you."

I cupped his jaw, letting him read it in my eyes, in the way my body moved against his. "Let me stroke your cock."

He stilled just for a second. As if he'd never heard the word uttered with reverence, command, and laughter all tangled into one. Something wild and terrified crossed his face before the scale-armor settled, and he nodded once, regal, shattering.

I wrapped my hand around his length, mapping heat and pulse and the alien flex of living flesh beneath my palm. His head lolled back, exposing the corded strength of his neck, throat working over a choked sound. "Stars above."

The ridged lip at his glans suckled greedily at my thumb, as if learning me in return, hungry, alive. I stroked him from root to quivering tip. The lubricant he produced was thick, sweetly metallic, slicking my palm. Every pass made him twitch, body threatening to shatter the sleeping platform beneath us. He made no move to control me. He just ... gave himself, every pant and shudder and convulsive tremor a submission I'd never dared win from anyone.

He caught my wrist, not to stop my hand, but to ground himself, his enormous thumb circling my pulse, claiming it as his own. *"Veshari—"* Raw, guttural. Like he was reciting a prayer with every syllable.

I watched the way he trembled, how he flayed himself open under touch. Power and surrender, the intoxicating knowledge that the most lethal creature I'd ever met was vibrating with pleasure because of me.

Need coiled in my gut, sharp as fear and just as sweet.

His tail slid between my thighs again, still slick from my own climax, curling possessively around my leg as if to anchor us both. He slid his hand over mine, pumping furiously until he came with a groan, cum spilling out over my hand and dripping down onto my thigh.

We froze, him arched above me, head thrown back, jaw clenched so hard the cords of his throat stood out like cables. I watched his face as he let go, the gold of his eyes eclipsed by black, stunned, unguarded, more animal than man. Hot, viscous seed painted my knuckles and my thigh in thick, shimmering ribbons. His release was heavy, wild, tinged with that sharp, metallic-spice scent that had threaded through every fight, every moment of tension between us, now concentrated, intoxicating.

He sagged, breath ragged on my cheek as he braced himself over me, his sweat-slicked chest shuddering with each inhale. His tail coiled tight around my calf, flexing, still claiming, still anchoring. I traced the delicate cracks in his scales, feeling the heat radiating off him, heat I'd fed, stoked, dared into eruption.

For a beat, nothing existed but the aftermath: the sticky wet between my thighs; the way his chest rose and fell, brushing my breast with every exhale.

Zarvash shifted, careful, easing his weight off mine but keeping an arm across my waist, his tail a loose, possessive loop. I stared at the ceiling, counting long cracks, marking time by every hitch in his breath. The air was thick with us, with what we'd done, with the promise of more and the certainty that nothing in this broken city would ever be the same.

Neither of us spoke. There was nothing to say.

For now, his body was a shield, his breath anchored to my skin, and the world beyond the bolted door could burn.

I SLUNK through the guts of the arena, shadows clinging to me like cobwebs. Above, the roar was a physical thing. Every cheer, every gasp – a story ending in someone's blood soaking the sand.

And Zarvash was up there. Fighting for his life.

The thought made something clench tightly in my chest. Sharp. Unwanted. I shoved it back. *Focus on the mission. Find the humans. Get intel.* That's why I was down there, risking my neck. Not to agonize over a Drakarn warrior who could handle himself.

Even if I could still feel the imprint of his mouth on mine, feel his body pressed against my skin. Damn it, I didn't need the distraction.

There were three identical hellmouths as the corridor split ahead of me. I froze, ears straining.

Left: the faint, rhythmic clang of metal on metal. The armory? Right: just darkness thick enough to swallow you whole and the plink-plink-plink of dripping water. Straight ahead ... voices. Hushed. Hurried.

Human.

My gut tightened. I pressed myself to the clammy wall, holding my breath, skirting the puddles gleaming on the floor. One wrong step ... The voices sharpened. A man. A woman. English. Fast. Scared.

"... can't just sit here waiting to die," Kinsley rasped. "If they pick one of us for tomorrow's 'entertainment'—" Her voice cracked.

"And what choice do we have?" Asif. His tone was flat, dead. "Last time someone got brave, three of us ended up decorating the sand. Or did you forget that?"

I rounded the corner, slow and careful. They were cowering in a reeking alcove, hemmed in by buckets and bloodstained rags. Kinsley, on her knees, scrubbed rust-colored stains from some piece of arena gear. Asif sifted through a pile of dented, broken armor like a vulture picking at bones.

They spotted me and froze. Pure, animal terror flared in their eyes before a flicker of recognition doused it. Barely.

"You." Kinsley's whisper was a puff of air, her brush clattering to the stone. "Are you insane? If they find you down here *again*—"

"I can handle myself." We didn't have time to argue about my habit of wandering.

Asif shot a terrified glance down the corridor, his Adam's apple bobbing. "Your ... *master* ..." He choked out the word. "Does he know you're here?"

Master. Right. The word scraped down my spine like a Drakarn's claws. "He's a little preoccupied at the moment," I said, keeping my voice level. "I thought we could talk."

Kinsley's eyes, already hard, narrowed to slits. "About what? You've seen this shithole. What more is there to know?"

"How many of you are there?" I had to fight the urge to snap. "Total. Here in Ignarath. Or beyond, if you've heard anything."

They traded a look. The kind that said, *do we trust her?* Asif let out a breath that carried the weight of the world. "Twenty-three. That we know of. Eight here in this godforsaken arena, us five in general service, plus the three ... collaborators." His lip curled. "Seven at the pleasure dens. Another eight at the mining camp east of here. There used to be more of us."

My heart gave a painful thump. "They're ..."

Kinsley nodded, a flicker of something—sympathy?—in her eyes. "Dead."

"The rest of our ship?" I pushed, dread coiling in my stomach. "Do you have any idea what happened?" One minute I'd been in cryosleep, the next I'd woken up on Volcaryth. I didn't know if it was a mechanical malfunction that had brought us down or something else.

"They're dead," Asif said, the word a stone dropping into a well. "Or scattered so far across this hell-planet they might as well be."

I didn't want to believe it, but there was no use pressing yet. "What about—"

A shadow slammed down, swallowing the meager light in our alcove. My hand snapped to the knife hidden under my tunic. Every muscle in my body screamed, coiling tight. Fight or flight.

Always fight.

"What are you doing down here?" The voice was deep. Dangerous.

I spun and damn near swallowed my tongue.

Omvar. The red behemoth from the feast.

Up close, he wasn't just imposing; he was a walking mountain range. Eight feet of crimson-scaled muscle that seemed to suck the air out of the space, his scales catching the dim light like polished bloodstones. And those eyes, molten gold, pinning me with an intensity that made my skin crawl. Pure predator.

Kinsley and Asif hit the dirt like they'd been poleaxed, foreheads to the grimy stone. Submission. Smart. Me? I stood my ground, knife halfway out but still hidden under my tunic, my brain screaming odds that were laughably bad. Not good? Try suicidal.

"Please stand," he told the other humans. "There's no need for that. I didn't mean to interrupt."

My throat was dry. "Uh, we're fine," I managed, forcing the words out past the lump. "I was asking them for directions. This place is a bit of a maze." True enough.

A flicker at the corner of his massive mouth. Almost a smile. "Indeed. I'll lead you back to where you're supposed to be. Skorai's guards are on the war path today. You'll be safe with me."

Tension ratcheted up, thick enough to choke on. Strike now? No, he'd crush me.

"Come," he said. "Your master's match is about to begin. I'm sure he'd want you there to witness it."

I risked a glance at Kinsley and Asif, still plastered to the floor.

"They won't be punished," Omvar said, gaze sharp. "Not by me. But you need to leave. Now."

No choice. Not if I wanted them, or me, to see another sunrise.

"Fine."

Omvar's claws, surprisingly gentle for their size, closed around my upper arm. Firm, though. No escape. He wasn't dragging, more ... guiding. As we left the alcove, I glanced back. Kinsley and Asif were watching, faces a mess of fear and something else I couldn't quite decipher.

Pity? Maybe. Or relief.

He led me up a spiraling series of corridors, closer and closer to the arena's roar. Guards snapped to attention as he passed. Warriors dipped their heads. Slaves practically melted into the walls. Yeah, this Drakarn was a big deal. Great.

"You're either very brave or very foolish," he said finally, the silence stretching thin.

"I don't know what you're talking about," I muttered, playing dumb. It rarely worked.

He snorted. "The Scalvaris warrior claimed you. Saved your pretty human hide. And here you are, poking around Ignarath with a sharp stick every chance you get. Why?"

I didn't answer right away. How much to give

this giant red question mark? "They're my people," I said, the truth plain and simple.

"Ah." A slow nod, like that explained the universe. "Loyalty. A commodity in short supply in this city."

We burst into blinding sunlight. The roar of the crowd hit me like a punch. Omvar steered me toward a raised section, prime seating for elite warriors and their ... trophies. Perfect. A front-row seat to whatever fresh hell was brewing.

"Your warrior fights Dravka next," Omvar rumbled as we settled onto cold seats. "He'll need every scrap of skill just to breathe by the end of it." Cheery bastard.

My eyes scanned the sun-blasted sand and found Zarvash easily. A statue of bronze scales and glinting fury at one end of the oval, his face a mask of cold, locked-down determination. Across from him, his opponent. Dravka. Scales the color of a deep bruise, a purple that was almost black. Even from there, the malice rolled off him in waves.

This wasn't sport. This was murder waiting to happen.

"What's his story?" I asked, my voice tighter than I wanted.

"They call him The Viper," Omvar replied. "He

loves dirty tricks. Poison. Mind games. Likes to draw things out. Make them scream."

A cold fist clenched in my gut. "Poison? That's allowed in this circus?"

Omvar's jaw tightened, a ripple under his scales. "No. But proving it? That's another thing entirely. Accusers tend to have ... unfortunate accidents."

The horn blared. Match on.

Zarvash and Dravka circled warily, weapons out. Zarvash moved with that lethal grace I was starting to recognize, his injured wing strapped tight, blade a sliver of deadly light. Dravka was ... different. Sinuous. Hypnotic. Twin daggers wove patterns in the air, catching the sun.

"Your master fights well," Omvar observed, his tone unreadable. "For a grounded beast."

My teeth ground together. "He's fine."

"A Drakarn who cannot fly is like ..." He paused, searching for a term. "A bird with clipped wings. Still capable of a nasty peck, perhaps. But fundamentally broken."

"He already won once," I bit out.

"Indeed." Omvar gave me a long, assessing look. "Tell me, little human, how many of your kind does Scalvaris shelter?"

Casual. Too casual. That had to be a trap. "I

wouldn't know," I said, making my face a blank mask. "Zar— My master found me outside the city, remember?"

"Of course." His lips twitched. He didn't believe a word.

On the sand, the dance had turned deadly. Dravka lunged in a purple blur. Zarvash dodged, a hair's breadth from getting his throat slit. The crowd gasped. My heart threatened to explode. He countered, blade flashing, forcing Dravka back. Metal shrieked against metal.

I hated this.

"Scalvaris is ... a strange place," Omvar continued, gaze fixed on the fight. "A city buried deep in the earth, hiding its secrets from the sky."

Before he could say more, there was a collective *hiss* from the crowd. My eyes snapped back to the arena.

Dravka. He'd scored a shallow cut on Zarvash's forearm. It shouldn't have been anything. But Zarvash recoiled, face twisting in a flash of agony. Staggered.

"Poison," Omvar spat, his voice suddenly hard. "The coward."

Zarvash recovered, but he was slower. Less fluid. The crowd smelled blood, the cheers turning uglier, more frenzied. Whispers slithered through the stands.

"Do you know what he used? Is there an antidote?" I asked, voice tight, strained.

Omvar nodded, grim. "Yes. If he survives the match."

If.

The word hit me like a stone to the chest. I gripped the edge of the stone seat, knuckles white. Zarvash fought on, pure grit, but every move cost him. Sweat gleamed on his bronze scales.

Dravka, the bastard, pressed his advantage. Bolder now. Cruel. Toying with him. Drawing it out. For the crowd. For his own sick kicks.

"Come on," I breathed. "Fight, you scaly asshole. Fight."

As if he'd heard me. Zarvash exploded. No more defense. Pure, reckless offense. Brutal. Direct. He caught Dravka off-guard, the purple warrior scrambling back, surprise momentarily wiping the smirk off his face.

Zarvash battered Dravka across the sand, blade a whirlwind. The crowd went insane. For a heartbeat, I thought he had him.

Sheer will. Sheer fury.

Then disaster. Dravka feinted, a blur. Then a

vicious kick. Right into Zarvash's bound, injured wing. I heard the crack. Sickening. Even over the roar. Zarvash went down hard. A scream of pure agony ripped from his throat.

The crowd erupted in bloodlust as Dravka moved in for the kill.

"No!" The word tore out of me, and I barely recognized my own voice.

But Zarvash wasn't done yet. Dravka loomed, blade high for the final flourishing blow. He wanted to show off. And that was his undoing.

Zarvash's tail, thick as my arm, lashed out and swept Dravka's legs. The Viper crashed to the sand.

In an instant, Zarvash was on him. A bronze thunderbolt, fury incarnate. His blade was at Dravka's throat, drawing a thin, dark line. Not deep enough to kill.

Not without permission.

Silence. Absolute. The arena held its breath.

All eyes swung to Skorai's pavilion. His call. Death or mercy.

The moment stretched into eternity. Then Skorai's hand, horizontal. Turned. Upwards. Mercy. A groan from some, cheers from others.

Blood denied.

Zarvash pushed himself back, blade still up.

Wary. But Dravka, beaten, slowly raised his hands in surrender.

It was over. He'd won.

Relief hit me so hard I swayed, the world tilting. My lungs, which had apparently forgotten how to work, suddenly dragged in a shuddering breath.

"Impressive," Omvar said, something like genuine admiration in his voice. "Your warrior has more fight and luck than I credited."

I barely registered his words. My gaze was locked on Zarvash. Limping from the arena. Stiff with pain. Blood seeping from a dozen places. Face a mask of agony, but his eyes ... even from there, I saw the fire. Triumph.

He'd survived. Thank the fucking stars.

"I need to see him," I said, already pushing to my feet. "Now."

Omvar nodded, rising with a grace that belied his bulk. "Follow me. I know the way to the fighters' pens."

We shoved through the exiting horde, Omvar a living battering ram. Guards melted aside. Doors opened. His presence was a key.

The fighters' chamber was a long, stone-lined room, echoing with groans and the clatter of medical tools. Alcoves held the day's casualties. Most already attended. At the far end was Zarvash. Alone. He sat on a stone bench, fumbling with a bandage one-handed.

I was across the room before I knew I'd moved, all pretense of "pet" gone. "Stop that. You'll make it worse, you idiot."

He looked up. Surprise warred with pain on his battered face. "*Vesh*— Vega."

My eyes scanned his injuries. Alarm bells screamed. The arm cut: inflamed, angry red streaks radiating out. Poison, no doubt. Shoulder: hanging wrong. Dislocated. Bruises blooming like ugly flowers. A deep gash on his thigh still weeping blood.

"Where's the healer?" I demanded, looking around the chamber. The other fighters had attendants, but Zarvash was conspicuously neglected.

"Ignarath hospitality," he said with a bitter laugh that turned into a wince. "Enemies of the city receive ... minimal care."

"That's barbaric," I spat.

"That's politics." He shifted, trying to find a less painful position, and failed. "I've had worse."

"Liar."

Omvar appeared beside us, his massive frame blocking the light.

I turned to him, desperation overriding caution.

"Can you help? Is there someone you trust? A healer who won't just finish what Dravka started?"

Omvar considered this, his golden eyes unreadable. "There is … someone. Not official, but skilled. She treats those the arena healers won't touch."

"Take us to her," I demanded, not caring how it sounded. "Now."

WAKING UP HURT.

For a second, I floated on the edge, caught between memory and nausea, and then everything dropped. Awareness slammed in—battered bones, heat radiating out of my useless wing, fists clamping down on the sides of my skull.

I didn't smell blood, small mercies. It was something herbal and sharp. Like dirt after rain and old roots. The smell of life and healing.

I wasn't in the arena anymore.

Vague memories flashed through the back of my mind. Vega hauling me out as I stumbled across the sand, a large Drakarn I didn't know at her side.

Something dark and possessive lit up inside, and I had to bite back a growl. I fought the instinct. Jealousy was useless, especially now.

I didn't recognize the room. I flexed my claws and waited for some sign of trouble.

Nothing.

I was on a pallet of some kind, only a little softer than my normal sleeping platform. It was stuffed with battle moss, soaked and pressed until it could sap out the fever from a dying Drakarn. That stuff wasn't cheap. My wing throbbed, deep and old instead of the burning knife agony I had been getting used to. I had definitely been seen by a healer.

How?

The end of the match with Dravka was a blur.

Cuts and scrapes. Burning pain.

Poison?

For a second, I braced myself to sit. My head spun, but I pushed through it. The room swam in and out, shelves stacked with jars and little vials shoved up against the walls, ropes and bits of bones decorating the place. There were dried herbs rustling above a slit window, just enough to let in a bit of outside light.

And tucked in her own little nest of blankets in the corner was Vega, limp, half curled like she had collapsed in the midst of defending me. One arm was flung out over her eyes. Her body was tight, never quite relaxed. Every muscle was waiting for the next threat to make her spring awake.

Even unconscious, I would bet on her against any opponent.

Quick and stupid relief washed over me. She was safe. The kind of concern I felt for her made me weak, but I couldn't avoid it. It was ridiculous. I shoved the feeling into a box and almost missed the door creaking open at the other side of the room.

A Drakarn female, stocky with drooping wings, swanned in. She had dark scales, old scars, and a bearing that made her seem twice as tall as she was.

Even in Ignarath, a healer's attitude was the same.

She dropped a tray with enough force to rattle my teeth, broth, a battered pouch, and she had a glare worthy of an executioner. "The dead man wakes," she drawled, not bothering to check if I was about to attack her.

That seemed a little rude. I was a warrior, after all, and quite a good one.

I tried to straighten, failed. "I remember the pit, the poison." Everything in my mind scrambled. "After that?"

She poked my wing, and I hissed in pain. She pulled the bandages back and checked the wound. I saw goo the color of sludge that was leaking under my scales. It didn't hurt much. I was mostly numb.

"You'd have been food for the rats if she hadn't dragged you here." A jerk of her chin at Vega. "And this wing ..."

I flinched. "It works." I flexed the limb anyway, half daring it to give out on me.

She snorted. "Until it doesn't. If your pet had waited any longer to bring you here, you might have lost use of it for good."

"Don't call her that," I snapped.

I was in too much pain to keep up the ruse.

Vega was so much more to me than a pet, and I knew what the Ignarath thought of humans. I couldn't keep the mask.

The healer raised a brow. "Yes, that she is, strange to see from a warrior in the tournament."

"I have a life outside of the pit."

"You certainly don't sound like someone from around here." She paused and waited for me to take the bait. When I didn't, she shrugged. "The herbs I've given you will fight the infection and mend the flesh, but you need to let it rest."

I didn't like the sound of that. "How long?"

"A week at least." From her expression, it was clear she wanted to tell me to wait longer but knew I would ignore anything worse. "If you push it, I won't be able to fix it again."

No sympathy, just flat truth.

I gritted my teeth. "I'll be as careful as I can." But there were more matches to come, more fights, and Vega and I would have to get out of Ignarath somehow. My wings needed to work.

She just snorted. Clearly, she'd dealt with warriors before. So why was she in some dim little quarters instead of plying her trade for the fighters flush with coin who needed tending?

She edged closer, dropping her voice. "That one threatened to gut my assistant if we so much as took a wrong step. She nearly bit me, a fierce one, huh?"

It twisted something in my chest, irritation, pride, something very messy. Something I couldn't let myself name. "Do you have a name?"

"Kazidee."

I would remember it. "You have my thanks for your healing, but I have no coin to pay you." I'd earned a little from the first match, but it was difficult to bet on myself when I didn't know the bet makers in town. And I didn't know the rest of the fighters well enough to risk making any official bets on them.

Vega and I could feed ourselves, and we had the room, but that was about it.

Kazidee leveled a hard look at me. "It's been taken care of. Don't worry about it. Now eat and stay still while I tend to you. Don't mess up my work."

She glared at me, as though waiting for me to argue. I didn't; I was too tired. Even just sitting up had taken it out of me. I had a fight tomorrow.

How was I going to be ready?

It didn't matter. I had to be.

Kazidee huffed and started sorting her herbs, dropping some into the broth on the tray before handing it to me.

"What are you giving him?" Vega asked, sitting up from her pile of blankets.

"The guard beast awakens," Kazidee muttered. "Healing herbs, broth. If you want him in fine shape, let me do my work."

Kazidee shoved the bowl at me. I picked up the broth and drank it down before Vega could make any sort of objection. After the first sip, I nearly coughed it back up. "It's spicy," I heaved, tongue recoiling.

"You will survive, warrior," said Kazidee.

"You seem like a pretty good healer," said Vega. "Why did I have to bring him to the outskirts of town to find you? I would think you could get work near the arena."

Kazidee stood and gathered everything but the

bowl of broth. "Learn to be thankful, outlander. My affairs are none of your business. Finish the broth and wait until his strength returns. It should be another couple of hours. Then be gone from this place."

She left us alone in the room.

"You found a healer," I said.

"I did." Vega leveled a stare that dared me to speak against it.

"It was a risk coming to her." We were in the city for a reason, and I was in the tournament under false pretenses. Our luck with Skorai would run out soon. And Kazidee could be running back to the arena right now to report on my injuries. It would be worth a fair bit of coin to my next opponent.

But I was already feeling stronger. My cuts looked days old instead of hours, and my wing hurt less than it had since the battle outside of Scalvaris.

"It was a risk we had to take," she said. "Or did you want me to let you die of Dravka's poison?"

I made enough room for her on the pallet and patted the sheets beside me. "Come up here. Sit."

"You will let your *pet* into your bed?" She raised her brows and pursed her lips.

"Don't," I said.

I thought Vega might argue. It was what she was made to do.

Instead, she stalked forward those few steps and slid into the bed, curling herself in right next to me. Muscles I hadn't realized I was clenching loosened.

This was it. Now she was where she belonged.

I finished the spicy healing broth and set the bowl aside. "You should try to sleep," I told my mate.

"I slept," she insisted.

Whatever she'd been doing, I doubted it was restful, but I didn't argue. We sat there like that for a long time. And eventually I could hear the sounds of the city outside. It must have been daytime. My match had been in the morning, and I wasn't fighting until evening tomorrow. Hopefully, it would be enough time to recover.

I must have dozed in the warmth of her presence. I drifted, half-aware, as the hush in the room stretched on. Outside, the normal thrum of Ignarath carried through the stone, merchants haggling, the distant bark of orders, the occasional clatter of armored boots along the streets.

At first, it was only background noise; the city's pulse steady and reliable. But slowly, the pitch shifted. Voices grew sharper, the footsteps heavier, something urgent bleeding through the cracks. Vega stiffened beside me, both of us attuned to trouble even through exhaustion. A strange hush spread as if the air itself held its breath, and I felt that old, primal surge: the forewarning of danger.

I wasn't surprised when Kazidee burst back into the room.

"You two need to get out of here now. Guards from the upper city are causing trouble. You don't want to be found with me." She thrust a bag full of herbs at Vega and shoved us towards the door. "Morning and night in his tea, if you want him to survive."

THE DOOR SHUDDERED as I slammed it, the frame quivering with the violence coiled under my restraint. Bolt drawn, one more fragile barrier pressed between the city's threats and my fraying composure.

We'd slipped past the guards and whatever trouble they brought. Poison burned along my nerves, my injured wing a dull throb with every movement. But then there was that memory. The dark haze of a thought that was trying to surface as my body healed. Her, pressed next to a crimson scaled brute of a warrior.

Who was he? Why?

Vega was already at the window, scanning the alley with a warrior's vigilance, wild hair framing a face cut sharp with adrenaline. Dust smeared her brow, sweat glazed her skin, and beneath the scent of fear twined that heady, familiar part of her that made me yearn, brighter, sharper in the aftermath of danger.

I couldn't bury the question any longer. "How did you find the healer?" My voice came out grating, too harsh. Every muscle in me strained against the urge to pace, caged, unworthy, half-mad with feelings I could not voice.

She shot me a look that would have skinned a lesser creature. "A Drakarn named Omvar knew her. He seems ... I don't know if I'd call it nice, but a possible ally. He protected one of the humans at the feast from a handsy asshole. But he tried to stop me from snooping in the arena. I don't know if it was out of a misguided sense of helping or if he didn't like the sight of me. You needed a healer, and it wasn't like I could ask Skorai. I took a chance."

A spike of jealousy shredded my restraint. My claws curled tight. "You trusted a champion of Ignarath?" My tail lashed once, a warning pulse through the room and through me. Even now, something heated deep in my skin, a reflex as old as the clan wars, rage and longing twisted together whenever I imagined another's scent on her skin.

She shrugged, all play and provocation. "Did you

expect me to turn down help because he's taller than you?"

A snarl rumbled up from somewhere deep, unbidden. Instincts strained beneath my skin: mark her, shield her, drive off rivals, never let her forget who she belonged to.

My wings flexed, tail flicking, pain be damned.

There was a feral spark in her eyes that told me she saw everything. "Is that it? Are you ...? You can't be jealous."

Her words needled deeper than I wanted to admit. I prowled closer, closing the space between us until there was nothing but a breath. "I'd tear the heart from any Drakarn fool enough to try harming you." My voice ran ragged, an oath and a plea all tangled up together.

Her eyes glinted, bright with hunger and something almost uncertain. "Why? I'm just ..."

I halted, letting my shadow spill across her. My fangs throbbed, tongue prickling with the sharp taste of her want, and under all the fury, need lurked, swift and dizzying.

"Just? You are *just* nothing." My words rasped raw. All I wanted was to prove my claim, but also, by the Forge I wanted to ask for hers, to see myself reflected in the heat of her gaze. "Do you want to see how far I'd go if another male dared touch you?"

Her bravado flickered. "Why?" she asked again.

Her word hit with the force of a storm, stripping my soul to unvarnished want. The shell of jealousy splintered, spilling out pride, anger, fear, and most of all longing so sharp it made my scales ache. My cock filled, heat leaking out, scenting the air, begging for sanctuary, and drinking her in.

I caught her wrist, careful with my claws, determined, reverent. I turned her palm upward, searching for the frantic flutter of her pulse, and dragged a line with my claw from wrist to the tender crook of her elbow.

Just a whisper of touch, a promise.

A plea.

She trembled beneath my hand, breath stuttered.

On impulse, I dropped to one knee, pressing my nose into the hollow there, letting her fill my lungs, dirt and iron, fear, defiance, but at the very heart, the wild honey-bright warmth that was only her. I licked her skin through a tear in her tunic, a trail of heated devotion, willing her to taste the words I could not utter aloud.

She gasped, hips arching toward me. "Zarvash—"

My vow was a snarl against her flesh. "I would

raze the arena to dust, rip every champion apart to keep you safe. For a single mark upon you, I would burn every stone in this cursed city."

She tilted her chin, a warrior's challenge, and the most fragile surrender. "Prove it, then."

Her want was a dare. Every battle faded, leaving only us, bonded by wounds, by desire, by all that had not yet been spoken.

I lifted her, cradling her thighs around my waist, and carried her to the battered sleeping platform. She laughed, wild and bright with the kind of joy born from mortal danger and hard-won trust, the kind of laughter that braided hope into the marrow of my bones.

I eased her onto the rough bedding, following with a knee between her thighs. My tail wound around her ankle, not claiming, but promising, my strength was hers, my body a bulwark against the world's cruelties. My cock ached, glands pulsing and heating. The musky perfume of Drakarn want hung like incense, more than claim: this was a prayer.

I tore at my tunic, claws slipping in urgency, the ache of wounds replaced by a sweeter agony. She wrestled with stubborn knots and grimy fastenings, her hands skimming my scars, her touch a challenge and comfort. Survival had left its marks on us.

She tossed aside her tunic, shoulders bare and dusted with freckles, every faded scar a story of strength. I nearly reeled at the sight. Her body was beautiful and flawed, more gorgeous than any star-strewn sky, closer than blood.

She shed her trousers until only a battered scrap of underwear hid the sweetest secret of her form. She met my stare, daring, trembling, radiant. Without breaking eye contact, she drew the final garment down, baring herself utterly.

"Is there anything here you want?" she taunted softly.

I knelt, overcome. "Everything."

I straddled her, bronze scales against delicate human skin. Her hands mapped my chest, tracing the old wounds, the new lines written atop them. I pressed my face to her throat, inhaling where her pulse thudded wild.

I let hunger rise in my voice, truth and worship entwined. "*Veshari.*"

My cock brushed her thigh, painting her skin with the sharp, smoky essence of my longing. I let myself scentmark her hips, her belly, the tender skin below her ribs because to deny that urge would rip me in half.

She arched, grinding up, inviting more, the

crown of my cock sliding through slick heat, separated only by bravado and the hush between heartbeats. "If you want me, fucking take me."

Her challenge undid me.

With a flick of my tail, I coaxed her knees apart, circling under to cradle her hips, lifting her open. She watched me, unafraid, every inch offering itself for worship.

I pressed my cock, the scales of its root, the barely yielding tip, along her folds, letting my musk mingle with her own. At the tip, the sensitive lip rippled of its own will, caressing her enough for us both to gasp. But I pulled back. It wasn't time for that yet. Not when I needed the taste of her.

"Let me see you." My voice was gruff as I nuzzled lower, dragging my tongue down the soft line of her stomach. "You carry the taste of battle, and you are so very ready for me."

She set her jaw, almost insolent, vulnerable. "Is it enough for you?"

I let my grin flash, a warrior's confidence, a lover's awe. "It is more than enough."

I parted her further, savoring how every pulse spoke of trust. My tongue, broad and hot, drew a slow line up her most sensitive seam. She bucked, shivered, hands flying to my head, grasping for horns I no longer had, clutching my hair instead.

My tail pressed against her, teasing the entrance, flicking and pulling at her clit and inner heat all at once. She writhed, a holy storm of need and delight, but never sought to flee.

"What— What are you—?" she gasped.

I rumbled my assurance into her flesh. My tail pulsed within, stroking with intoxicating precision, while my tongue danced in counterpoint.

Her thighs pressed my head, body bowing from the bed in shock. Pressure built between us, fury and gentleness entwined, until she shattered around my mouth, sobbing my name. It was a song of victory and surrender.

Still, I lapped at her, drawing every last aftershock forth until her hands, frantic, batted at my shoulders. "Enough. Zarvash—don't. I need. God, let me breathe."

I looked up, triumphant and humbled by her sweetness. My chin and jaw gleamed with her pleasure; my cock was a column of fire against her thigh.

She pulled me up, her mouth fierce, lips devouring the last traces of her taste from me. She was wild now, wanton, her grip on me urgent and sure. My shaft throbbed against her belly. Her hands explored, fingertips a delight as they traced scales, ridges, veins. Her thumb stroked the lip at the tip, drawing out another string of hot, heady slick, tasting me with every pass.

"You are fucking amazing," she murmured, hunger and awe blending. "I want to know you're real."

She pressed me down, taking her place above me for a moment, testing both her power and my trust. Her tongue ran the length of my throbbing cock, and as she drew the crown into her mouth, the lip caressed her in turn, a wordless exchange, my gift for hers.

I trembled, tail flailing against bedding, claws scraping for anchor. "Keep that, and I will fall, *veshari*."

She paused, wicked satisfaction softening her smile. "Do you want me to stop?"

"If you leave me wanting, I will never forgive you."

She drew me deeper, savoring, until my control frayed. I caught her hand, not to stop her, but to save some last remnant of self.

She tasted victory and let me pull her astride me, straddling my waist, her hair wild, her eyes molten and inescapable.

She angled me to her center, the lip at my tip stroking, beckoning, pledging. I steadied her hips, guiding without force, letting her take as much as her body would allow. Inch by slow inch she sank over me, a sacred joining—her velvet heat stretched, enfolded me, claimed me in return.

"Oh, God—" Her words dissolved in sighs.

I thrust gently, fighting the wildfire urge to lose myself, savoring her every wince and whimper, her pleasure-twisted features the most beautiful sight in all the world. The lip at my crown swirled within, stroking secret spots, coaxing more pleasure, coaxing more love.

She braced above me, riding slowly, her hands splayed on my chest, fighting for every ounce of control as desire warred with need. I caught her gaze, refusing to let this be anything less than truth.

"Say it," I begged, hardly more than a breath, not sure what I was truly asking.

She met me, spirit unbroken, pleasure blazing fierce as any flame. "Yes, please, cum in me. I need you."

Her words broke me. I surged up, hips meeting hers in a rhythm older than stone, cock jerking as her body clenched, surrendering to release once more. My tail circled her waist, drawing her closer, grounding us both in the holy tangle of flesh and longing and hope.

Her climax tore her name from my lips, a raw, wordless roar. I spilled into her, thick and unrestrained, marking her at every level, body and soul, our scents knitted now and forever in the air around us.

We held, trembling, my tail refusing to let her go, body shuddering with every aftershock. Her sweat streaked my scales, and her scent became my sanctuary.

Eventually, she eased off, collapsing at my side, thighs marked by our joining, stomach glittering with all we'd spent. I watched my claim seep into her skin, not a brand of dominance, but the most fragile, sacred contract, hers as much as mine.

I gathered her in, pressing my lips to her temple, breathing her in, sharing all that was fierce and all that was soft. "You are a danger I would face a thousand times," I murmured, "and I would choose you. Always."

Beyond the door, darkness lurked, echoes of shouts, the press of duty, and the arena's bloody challenges. But here, wreathed in the scent and heat of our union, there was only this fragile, precious hour.

I cleaned the last traces from her skin with my

tongue, savoring the taste of us, the way she shivered gently in my hold. When I wrapped my tail around her, it was not to claim, but to shield, to cradle all of her, for as long as fate allowed.

Her fingers twined through mine, silent, but so much passing between us.

Bond-words hovered, unspoken, on my tongue, in the echoing fullness of my heart. Not yet. But I would speak them.

Soon.

## ZARVASH

THE TASTE of victory soured quick in Ignarath. The corridor beyond the arena pulsed hot with old blood and fresh humiliation, dust grit grinding under my scales. I could barely feel the afterglow, only the ache in my side, a poison throb deep under bruised ribs, every breath a reminder I was still alive.

For now.

Guards herded me from the sand with dull nods, hands jittery for a fight even when the arena was done with me. Respect on their terms: given only to those too stubborn to die. I shrugged off the worst of the dust, worked my shoulder against the ache, eyes hunting for danger. The Ignarath never let an enemy forget where they stood; they paraded you, sometimes with banners, sometimes with knives.

Omvar stood in the crook of shadow and torchlight, impossible to miss. Red giant, bull-strong, his silhouette dwarfing the guards who pretended not to fear him. He pushed off the wall as I neared, torch glow flickering over the broad plane of his scaled shoulders.

"Not easy to kill, Scalvaris," he rumbled. No warmth, just respect hammered flat with caution, a threat and an invitation both. His gaze lingered just long enough on the blood at my elbow, the jagged cut trailing my jaw.

I showed teeth. "I'm still here." The words were dust and old wounds. This was the creature who'd helped my mate find a healer for me. Why? There was no room for friendship among champions, not when all that mattered was the blood on our blades and claws.

His snort was almost a laugh. "That you are." He jerked his chin, eyes following the distant echo of chaos. "Skorai must be waiting for you to stumble. He'd love to force you into his private fights."

A flicker of cold skittered under my scales. "He'll choke on my bones first." I kept my gaze flat, unreadable, measuring him even as pain howled behind my ribs.

He moved closer, his voice dropping. "Do you know how close that last match was?" He paused, head tilting just enough, a show of something almost like confession. "Some of us sleep better if our friends keep breathing."

Friends? I caught the word, searched it for venom. "Is that why you found the healer when my ... human asked?" I couldn't bring myself to use the other word. "Pet" was the label the city would carve on her collar—never on my tongue.

Omvar only shrugged, wings folded tight. "Everyone deserves a chance. She dragged you out of there and looked ready to gut anyone who got close. Hard to ignore courage like that." His eyes narrowed, testing. "You give her a lot of latitude."

"She knows her place." At my side. In my bed. Under my scales.

Forever.

And I could not show a hint of that there, even if Omvar seemed different from the other Ignarath.

Gratitude tried to rise, bitter and unwanted. "Thank you for directing her to the healer. Dravka had no honor."

The red beast scowled. "I won't pretend to be unhappy that you were the one to face him and not me." Sunlight licked red across his brow. "It's looking more and more like we'll face one another in the final round."

It was still days away, but Omvar had dispatched his opponents with ease. Like all of the matches, the final round was not necessarily to the death, but it ended in it more often than not. It was not unheard of for the champion to succumb to his wounds after victory. The funerals held in a fallen champion's honor were legendary.

I would not have one.

Vega and I needed to start thinking of our way out of this city. We knew there were humans there. We knew where they were kept. My wing was growing stronger by the day.

If we timed it right, Omvar might enter the champion's match to find the sands empty.

Enough speculation. Omvar's mouth twisted, his gaze hardening. "Your pet—" The word held no edge, just the warning of experience. "You need to be careful there. Skorai's dogs would cut her open for sport."

Every muscle clenched. "She is not—" The claim caught fire in my throat and died, strangled before I let it breathe. The ruse had been my idea in the first place. I couldn't abandon it now when it was the only thing protecting her in this damned city.

Omvar's eyes flickered. "She's ..." If he had something to say, it was swallowed by a commotion behind us.

Noise slammed into the hush of the corridor. Two guards stomped in, heavy-footed and grim, dragging a figure by the arms. Another Drakarn followed, reeking with aggression, a shredded blood-and-gold banner snarling against his back. The cloth was stained, edges ghosted with old violence. It was a war token. This was one of the champions I hadn't yet beaten. Rukos.

Let him rot.

My attention arrowed in on Vega.

I moved before thought, hackles up. She fought the guards, head high, jaw locked, mutiny burning in her bones. She looked every bit untamed and danger-ous. My pulse thudded hard in my neck. Then rage roared.

Rukos swept into the torchlight, arrogance coiled in every gesture. "This one," he spat, each word slick with venom, "forgets her place. She spits in the face of Drakarn authority."

Fury boiled under my mate's skin. She opened her mouth—

"Silence." My voice knifed out, cold and sharp. My hands trembled, not with anger but with calcula-tion. Omvar's warning echoed, hot and biting.

I crossed the space, closing the distance like a threat. The guards slunk aside, afraid, or wise enough to fake it. I latched a hand around Vega's shoulder and yanked her down onto the dirt at my feet. Pressed a boot between her shoulder blades. Not enough to bruise, a show, nothing more.

My tail looped her throat in a loose collar, a pantomime of restraint, breath and dignity untouched. She didn't struggle, just braced her hands to my tail, eyes snapping up in faked fury.

My pulse surged wild. Hatred for this performance, but more: the sick animal need to shield her from all harm.

The Ignarath champion swaggered forward, banner whipping over spiked scales, a brute whose hide still carried the shadow of every old wound. His fingers traced the chain at his belt like he was petting a weapon even though we were all unarmed.

"She insulted me. Slandered my victories," he growled, claws twitching, greed shining in his eyes. "I demand payment."

My stare narrowed. "Did she fail to bow? Are you so soft scaled?" I laced each word with acid. "Should I break her for calling you what you are?"

The corridor tensed. Every Drakarn poised, nostrils wide for blood.

Rukos lunged, snapping teeth, wings billowing with fury.

I let my teeth flash, a threat, a taunt. "Perhaps I should reward her for recognizing a coward."

He surged. Guards caught him, swinging him back behind their wall of spears. I dug my heel a fraction deeper into Vega, enough to send the right message—*mine*—without damage.

One guard hissed, "You must control your property, Scalvaris."

"The Tournament Master has made his displeasure clear," the other barked. "No more strays. Either keep your pet with you or lock it in the slave quarters while you're here. It is forbidden to wander."

Vega's hand squeezed my tail, twice. I understood the signal, even as it made bile rise in me.

I glared at the guards, voice low and lethal. "Then take her there. I'll collect her when I'm done with my business. Do not bother me with these useless things. But if she has a single bruise that I did not give her, I will demand payment in blood."

ROCKSLIDE. That's about how gentle the Ignarath guards were, only less thoughtful. They hauled me down corridors slick with the stench of fear and blood, claws digging into my arms with all the sympathy of a butcher inspecting a slab of beef.

"Move faster, slave." The guard had green scales, a roadmap of old scars, and eyes glazed with boredom and cheap cruelty. He shoved me hard enough that my teeth clicked, and I nearly bit my tongue. I stumbled, catching myself before I face-planted.

The corridor corkscrewed downward, light fading out in grudging increments the deeper they dragged me. Torches stuttered every few meters, casting thick shadows that pressed and squeezed, hungry and watching. Something dripped down the walls. I didn't check if it was water. It didn't exactly smell fresh.

We stopped at a door squatting at the end of the world. Wood reinforced by metal, rusty as an old nail. One guard fumbled for keys, the other kept his meat-hook grip locked on my arm, claws just shy of breaking skin.

"Your master will tire of you soon," green-scales sneered, hot breath slithering over my ear.

I gave him nothing, just the blank bored stare of a human with better things to do.

The door screamed on its hinges, opening wide enough for a slap of foul air to slap me full in the face. Unwashed bodies. Old waste. Hope abandoned at the threshold. Shoved hard, I went down, hands scraping against wet stone, grit grinding into an already growing bruise. Great.

"Enjoy your stay," the guard cackled, and then the door slammed behind me like a casket lid.

I waited there on the gross ground for three seconds. Let the echoes settle and the guards retreat before I slowly got up.

A cage. Stone walls wept. The floor was a slick, treacherous mosaic of who-knows-what. One torch guttered in a bracket too high to reach, coughing out more shadow than light. What a miserable place.

Over in the far corner: two figures huddled together. Kinsley was on her knees, working a filthy rag over someone's ruined face. Yelena. She had one eye swollen shut, her cheek splotched purple and black with a busted lip. Sweat pasted her hair to her skull. Her chest moved, barely.

Kinsley looked up at my approach, her expression wrapped in something tougher than exhaustion, resignation, bone deep. "Of course it's you," she whispered.

"What did they do to her?" I asked, picking my way across the uneven floor.

Kinsley's lips twisted, silent in a way that said more than words. She wrung pink out of the rag into a bowl that had maybe, once, hosted clean water. Yelena didn't move.

I made a circuit of the cell. The waste bucket reeked in one corner. Blankets thrown in a heap, threadbare and with more holes than fabric. A water basin that looked like someone had used it to rinse knives. The door behind me, solid, no easy escape. No windows. A vent in the ceiling, barely big enough for a skinny arm, if you could break every finger.

A tomb with a view of absolutely nothing.

Rounding back to Kinsley, I crouched. The light

wavered, shadowing her face, but not enough to hide the fine tremor in her hands. Up close, Yelena looked worse. The bruises on her neck were finger perfect. A chunk of her hair was torn away, scalp still angry red.

I started to ask something, but Kinsley hit me with a look sharp enough to draw blood. I swallowed the words, every useless question melting in the heat of her warning.

"If I can get you out," I said, low, pitching it for her, not the stones or any guard who might have prying ears. "We're looking at a month over rough terrain to get to Scalvaris. No bullshit. Who can actually do it?"

She sat back, hands knotted in that rag. Her gaze flicked to Yelena, grief in the set of her jaw, the furrow between her brows. Then back to me.

"Me. Asif. Maybe Nat." No apology. Just inventory.

Yelena's breathing evened, drifting, not sleep, more like the mercy of unconsciousness. Kinsley shook her head minutely, heavy with everything she wasn't saying.

"Don't talk about escape unless you mean it," she warned, voice brittle with the memory of too many lies, too many false hopes.

I drew in a breath, and it stuck halfway down my throat. "I'm working a plan. I don't have all the pieces yet." I couldn't make promises. "Are you in?"

Kinsley's hand hovered over Yelena's forehead, a tenderness practiced and worn. She reminded me a bit of Selene, but her edges were harder, honed on the terrors of Ignarath. "If we run, they'll punish everyone left behind."

"They didn't when Reika got out."

A spark in Kinsley's gaze. Was it hope? Fear? Both, probably. "She made it? Really?"

I nodded. "Yes." I shifted closer, keeping my voice low but urgent. "Scalvaris is ... well, it's still Volcaryth, so it kind of sucks, but it's nothing like here. It's a city built into a cave system with an underground river. They let us train with their soldiers. One of our people is training to be a healer." I hesitated, then added, "It's not perfect, but it's not *this*."

She stared me down for a beat, peeling back layers, searching for the fraud. "You trust these Drakarn?" Just a question, easy as poison.

Somewhere behind my ribs, memory flickered—Zarvash above me, scaled and burning-gold, filling me right to the breaking point, his tail tying me down at one moment and anchoring me in the next. The way he'd looked at me, like I was the only living thing in the universe. The heat clawed up my neck. Thank God for bad lighting.

"I trust Zarvash." My voice didn't shake. "With my life."

And my heart. My soul. I melted when he called me *veshari*.

And I suspected that I might know what it all meant. But Kinsley didn't need any of that. It might send her screaming into the depths of the city, never to return.

She weighed that then nodded. "God, I hope you're right."

"I am," I said, because this time there was no room for doubt.

MY WING THROBBED, joint stiff beneath the layered bandages, Kazidee's herbs still biting through my hide, leeching out the rot that tried to kill me from the inside. The memory of the arena fights clawed at the edges of my vision, Dravka's blades and claws.

But I was alive. And so was Vega.

We holed up in our bolted room, cramped, ugly, air soupy with sweat and fear. Vega sat by the door, every line of her a snare about to snap. She'd rigged a wire to the door latch and attached it to a clay pot. If someone messed with the door, it would drag us away the moment they tried their luck.

Sunlight highlighted her in slashes, gray stripes across her jaw and cheek. Even at rest, the tension coiled beneath her skin, all feral focus, nothing left for comfort. It set my nerves clattering; it made me want, more danger or more her.

More everything.

A dangerous game I was playing there. Nothing would make me stop.

She caught my look and turned. "You can stop brooding. If Skorai sends anyone through that door, I'll cut off their claws and make you a necklace of them."

She couldn't know what it would mean to wear my mate's war prizes around my neck. If she gave me such a gift, I would murder anyone who tried to take it from me.

I grunted and turned away, pacing the stripped floor, wings clamped tight against my aching side. My claws flexed, impatience burning through the pain of the healing herbs. I could feel Vega's silence, sharp, sliding between my ribs. Not accusation, not comfort. Something worse.

Finally, I had to speak. "You're planning to do something stupid." The words fell between us, pure challenge. My voice was stone.

Vega turned her head, eyes flat. "Stupid is in the eye of the beholder. You're the one fighting with that injured wing."

I folded my arms, careful not to show the twist in

my wing. "Two days. My wing will be ready by then. We fly. Just us. We can't afford anything else." It tasted bitter, too close to begging. "It's the only chance we get."

She smacked her hand against the sleeping platform, jaw tight enough to crack. "You want me to ditch the humans?" She spat the names like accusations. "Kinsley. Asif. Nat. Yelena. There's more! We just leave them? They won't last much longer."

I bared my fangs, not at her, not really, but at the world that kept demanding impossible bargains. "They won't last a day outside. The desert will strip them clean. If we take them, we risk everything." I risked *her*. Unacceptable.

Vega's mouth flexed in something like a snarl. "How Drakarn of you. If it was your people in those cages, would you be saying the same thing?"

For a heartbeat I pictured a cage full of desperate warriors, taken in battle or worse. I felt the weight of old wounds. Old guilt. I bit hard on my words; she'd struck true.

I looked away, claws flexing. My shadow pooled thick across the room, ugly, useless. "Carrying you will be risk enough."

Vega stood. Chin raised, flames in her eyes. She never flinched. Not for anyone. "And what about

Larissa?" Her voice dropped, blade sharp. "I don't know if Kira will survive if she knows we found her sister and left her in this cesspit."

I didn't answer. I didn't point out that we'd only heard of Kira's sister, that neither of us had laid eyes on her.

"I know you want them all," I managed, voice rough. "But if we play hero, we die. *You* die. I won't trade you for a handful of strangers. I wouldn't trade you for all of Scalvaris."

She sucked in a ragged breath, and her mouth stayed open in shock. "Zarvash …"

"For you," I said, clawing the words out. "For us. You are my first duty. I'm not burying you for anyone."

She stepped close, too close. I could smell her anger. Regret and wanting knotted together. My hand hovered, close enough to touch, to anchor her or myself, I couldn't say. Neither of us moved.

"I can't walk out of here empty handed," she whispered. "We've come this far. We have to do what we can to help, we need *proof*."

I gripped her wrist, claws gentle. Promise, warning, it didn't matter. We stood like that, silent, breathing in the cost of what trying truly meant.

"Anyone who proves they can run, who can fight.

If they keep pace … we try," I said at last, voice ironed flat. "But if they fall behind, we do not wait. As for the rest … we can't, *veshari*."

She shuddered. For a second, I thought she'd hit me, or bolt. Instead, she just shook her head. Drew herself together, angry as a wound. "It's the best we can do," she said, voice breaking, eyes fixed just below mine.

"It is," I bit out. Harsher than I meant. True anyway.

The words hung between us, all edges. Neither of us got what we wanted. I ached, not just from wounds. Choices always cost. Outside, bells tolled the hour; on the street, the drumbeat of feet, another patrol. Skorai was worried about something.

I flexed my wing, slow, steady, testing. Pain rose, sharp but not blinding. Two days, if luck held. We could wait that long. Hope was a needle, pricking holes in every plan.

I knelt by our battered pack. Flatbread, a half-filled waterskin, a knife. Pathetic. Not enough for two, let alone whoever we could rescue.

Vega stalked behind me, pacing, a storm condensed to fit inside her bones. "What if you can't fly?" she asked, all cool planning again, walling off the rawness.

"We find a way to sneak out. With more than the two of us, we'll have to do that anyway. At night, when the guards are in their cups or thumping skulls in the lower city." I pictured the place—the sticky dark, the stink—my map built by scent and scrape.

She weighed options, cold calculation flickering in her eyes. "We can use the matches as cover. Maybe. If you're not fighting." She dropped onto the sleeping platform, elbows pressed to her knees, head in her hands. "It's not even a shadow of a plan. But the first chance we have, we have to take it. We're about to wear out our welcome here."

Then, thud. Both of us shot up. Vega already had her blade in hand, eyes bright and hard. Bootsteps outside, heavy, armored, the wrong rhythm for a drunken sentry or cowed slave. I shifted, wing half-flaring despite the pain, turning to shield Vega out of instinct.

Three heartbeats, then a clean knock.

I unhooked the security wire. "Enter," I barked.

The door creaked slow to reveal a Drakarn, pale as winter in the far north, red tunic blazing, the silver chain of a herald too big for his neck.

He didn't meet my eyes.

"Zarvash, champion of the games," he intoned, voice dry as bones, "by Skorai's order, you are summoned to the Blood Hall at sundown for a mid-game celebration."

A sound vibrated in Vega's throat. She didn't like this. Neither did I.

But we were looking for our chance.

I bared my fangs. "And if I refuse?"

His gaze flicked up, blanched, dropped again. "Master Skorai has personally invited you, champion. It would be a great insult to refuse."

I let the silence stretch and watched him squirm. I had no desire to dance to Skorai's tune, to play the part of the perfect champion.

But I wasn't a fool, and I didn't have choices.

"I'll attend," I said.

He bowed, stiff as carrion, and fled, letting the door slam shut behind him.

PLANS WERE SUPPOSED to keep me sane. Keep moving, keep counting options, keep dragging everyone a step ahead of whatever nightmare wanted to eat us next. But by the end of our discussion, planning felt like gnawing on bone.

And now *this*. A feast to throw a wrench in our plans. Or to give us just the opportunity we needed.

But Zarvash's wing was still so weak. And I feared that Skorai was up to something. Why now with this feast? He couldn't possibly know what we were up to, not when the shape of the plan was only starting to form.

"This is our chance." I kept my voice steady. If I didn't believe in it, he'd never let me try. "You go to the feast. I get whoever I can to the east gate. We break out before dawn."

He didn't look hopeful. Zarvash melted into the shadow by the window, gold eyes molten, jaw set so hard I half expected scale to splinter. He could outstare stone.

"I'll be there. Don't try anything rash." Flat delivery, cold as obsidian.

It hurt, but I'd be lying if I said I didn't deserve it. I'd run off half-cocked from Scalvaris more than once, and it had only made things worse. This time, I had to work with him, to stick to the plan. Or we'd all end up dead.

The strangest thing was, there was no one on this planet—maybe in this freaking galaxy—that I trusted more.

Try telling that to the me from six months ago.

"Like you've got room to talk." I tried for a smirk, but it barely twitched across my mouth. This wasn't a joking matter.

That's the price of caring—worrying was a full-contact sport.

I squeezed his arm—something like a promise—then bolted before I could talk myself out of it. My heart rattled like small arms fire, all staccato and terror. Outside, the city was its same old toxic self, stone radiating blood warmth left by the suns, but the air tasted of rust, and smoke licked the wind from a dozen gutters. I kept to the alleys, melting into shadows wherever the city allowed.

Ignarath voices rolled ugly through the spreading darkness, the usual celebration of screaming and slaughter. Glasses shattered, laughter running knife-edged; it was enough. Drunk was distracted and distracted meant sloppy. Guards would screw up, wander off, maybe already half lit on the cheap booze in this part of the city.

I waited in the shadow of the booze and the guards. Zarvash would be inside by now. He had to play pretend and keep Skorai distracted. This time, I couldn't get caught. Before, it hadn't mattered, not truly. They'd return me to my "master" and let him mete out the punishment.

There was no room for that tonight. And Skorai was beginning to suspect something was up.

My hands didn't shake; they'd already passed into that fever calm where adrenaline wipes everything raw, though they ached for my knife. I'd mentally mapped every rat-run out; three options if you counted the sewers, which I did, even if it meant crawling through filth and nightmares.

If Kinsley and the others were locked in the pens

under the arena, I wouldn't have stood a chance. But it was my luck they were being used as servants tonight. The guards didn't pay me any mind as I slunk through the kitchens, shoulders slumped and whole demeanor screaming *submissive*. They saw a weak human in tattered clothes.

They needed to keep saying that.

Kinsley's eyes widened when she saw me. "Tonight?"

"Now." I kept my voice low. Drakarn servants were working in the kitchens, too, and I didn't trust them not to sound the alarm.

She didn't flinch. No pointless questions. I squeezed Kinsley's wrist and nodded to Asif. "What about Nat?"

I didn't see Yelena or Eli and didn't ask. I wasn't going to throw a wrench in the escape plan and invite hesitation.

"She's elbows-deep washing shit off plates," Asif said.

For a heartbeat, I just listened, far off, glass shattering, someone screaming not in fear but in wild, open-throated joy at the feast. Good. The more smoke and noise to cover us the better.

"We get her, and we go."

If Kinsley or Asif had a doubt, they didn't let it show. And regrets? Those weren't my problem.

Nat was at the cistern, hands scrubbed red and trembling around a bowl, scouring with a focus only pain could teach. Her arms looked like someone had tried to slice discipline into her skin. When our eyes met, hope and dread piled on top of each other behind her eyes.

"Come on," I said, voice just above a whisper. "It's time."

She set the bowl down, careful not to make a noise and nodded.

I gave her, Kinsley, and Asif my most confident nod. "Stay close. Fast and low. We don't look back."

I didn't let myself think about the people we were leaving behind. I could save who was in front of me—or at least I could try. If we got back to Scalvaris —*when* we got back—I'd plead with Darrokar on my life to go back for the rest, for Larissa. But we were all screwed if no one got out.

We vanished behind an old door that seemed half forgotten and led to a stinking hallway with wet floors and disgusting bugs skittering along the walls. I wasn't about to think about what was causing the stink, not when freedom lay at the end of the hall.

Nat nearly fell over, but Kinsley snapped a hand

out, teeth bared in a silent snarl, keeping her upright. Claws were in my lungs, sulfur on my tongue, every scrape of sound a potential death warrant.

At last, the hallway spat us out into fresh air, if you called a rancid alley "air."

I stopped and counted. I wasn't letting anyone fall behind just yet.

No alarms. No shouts. My hand locked white on my knife as I drew in slow breaths. "Come on, we need to get across the city."

Then the world snapped.

A muffled yell. Heavy, booted steps biting through mud. Then a dirty fan of torchlight slashing the dark, four Ignarath grunts boiling up from behind a barricade of splintered barrels.

"Escape!" The word landed like a mallet to the gut.

"Run!" My hiss shredded my throat. I was already gone.

Nat shot forward, Kinsley on her heels, arms pumping. Asif's hesitation cost him; hands like steel cable looped around his chest, yanking him back, his legs pinwheeling uselessly.

Kinsley pivoted with murder in her eyes, blade slashing fast and ugly. I lunged, but a guard's tail swept my shins. I ate dirt and something worse and came up spitting, jamming my knife upward into Ignarath flesh, hot, briny blood sprayed, guard howled.

A second's reprieve. Not enough.

Chaos swarmed. There was Nat, yanked back by her hair, shriek strangled to a whimper. Kinsley swearing, blade flashing, trying to carve through hides too thick for a kitchen knife. Asif vanished into a tangle of claws and fury, his shout snuffed like a candle.

I fought, bit, clawed, punched, headbutted until pain blurred into white static. Kinsley drove her heel into a guard's groin, bought herself a heartbeat before more claws crashed in, too many, too strong, all scales and bulk, every one twice my size.

"Go! Vega, just go!" Kinsley's scream was pure violence.

No!

We still had a way out, we had to. Nat was sobbing, Kinsley fighting like a monster. I launched at the next guard, barely thinking, knife jabbing, teeth bared, pure animal. An armored forearm erased my vision. A backhand snapped through my skull, bright light and fireworks inside my head.

Blindly, I swung, found something between soft and bone. Another grabbed my collar, hurling me

sideways, until I heard something pop. Kinsley materialized beside me, slashing wild, blood speckling her
fists.

"Get off her!" Her voice was breaking.

They replied with a roar, far past words, the
thrill of the hunt running riot in their eyes.

We went down swinging. The math was impossible. More boots. More metal. Somewhere in the
logic, I understood this was how it ended. Every
heartbeat dragged us deeper into defeat.

A guard's fist cracked into Kinsley's jaw and sent
her sprawling into the muck.

Then it was just me, arms yanked behind my
back, face mashed into gravel. Cold stone, blood in
my mouth. Overhead, a voice laughed, all rot and
satisfaction.

"You should've stayed in your cage, fragile prey."

I tried to snarl something, curse, promise
vengeance. All I got was black static at the edges.

Nat was screaming, then silence cut her off like a
knife.

Hands tore me upright, my shirt stretched to
ruin. The last thing I saw: Kinsley, limp but watching. Her one open eye burned straight through me,
all the things she'd never say. Sorry. Fury. Fuck this
place.

I tried to mouth something. Promise I'd get her out of this. That Zarvash would find us. That it would all be okay. But the dark swept in, fast, heavy as floodwater.

Noise. Pain.

Then nothing.

THE FEAST LAID itself bare like a slaughterhouse pretending to be a temple. Bowls of marrow, slabs of charred bird, crimson sauces slick as fresh blood, each dish sat in the flickering lamplight. The air groaned beneath the weight of oil, sweat, and too many warriors packed tight, their armor scraping warnings with every careless move.

Everything glittered. Gold, bone, jagged claws, ornaments sharp enough to cut, meant for admiration and threat. This was a gambler's feast.

And there sat Skorai, bloated with power at the table's head, layered in chains of office that bit into his scales. He drained his goblet again and again, as if he could swallow the dark itself and bend it to his will. Omvar loomed at his right, his form too broad for the gilded chair, arms folded as a living warning against insolence. I was on Skorai's left, caught between violence and vigilance, pinned under the weight of competing hungers.

Disgust curdled in my throat. Breathing itself felt like surrender.

Skorai's eyes twitched nervously from Omvar to me, searching for the weaker link. When a servant drifted too close, he hissed at me. "Where's your pretty, wild little human? Not animal enough to chew through chains, I hope. Wouldn't want her missing all this."

I bared my fangs, kept my tail languid in a show of indifference. "Chained in my quarters," I said, each word a deliberate, weighted lie. "She's more useful there than loose, snarling among soldiers."

The lie tasted foul. I wanted to think she was safe, but it was the furthest thing from the truth. She could do her job, I knew it. Something deep within me rebelled at leaving her out there alone.

Skorai sneered, only half satisfied. But I sensed the itch beneath his scales.

He craved something more, his gaze flickering over Omvar's silence like an addict deprived of a fix. Skorai wanted submission, but Omvar gave him nothing, merely stripped meat from bone in steady, unhurried motions. Frustration gathered behind

Skorai's smile, simmering with the tension of a blade held too long before battle.

I surveyed the room. Fallen champions devoured their food like victors. Guards clustered over dice games, their eyes darting our way when they thought we wouldn't see. Skorai's loyal dogs lined the walls, tense, unblinking. Every exit watched. Every avenue a trap, or an opportunity, if fate was playing nice.

Wine came. I sipped at my goblet and tipped as much out and onto the floor when no one was looking. I needed to keep my wits about me. Skorai raised his cup, savoring the pause he commanded.

"Tomorrow is the final trial," he announced, his voice wrapped in mock civility. "Two champions, one last dance in the sand. Until then, you sleep safe beneath my roof. No shadows, no assassins." His smile curved in a velvet-coated threat.

Refuse, and you were dead.

Omvar grunted. I inclined my head, offering nothing as much as I wanted to damn the man. Vega was out there without backup. The plan was to rendezvous, not spend the night in this serpent's den.

If I was to face anyone, I was glad it was Omvar. He was a worthy foe and an honorable Drakarn. I would have been happy to leave the victory to him by default, even if the fighting part of me wanted to test my claws against his. I would need to find a time to get away and find my mate.

I wouldn't leave her out there alone a second longer than I had to.

The night dragged. Skorai goaded, needled, seeking some crack in our armor. "Omvar, you've never had such a rough time in the games, have you?"

"Tell me, Zarvash, how did someone like you crawl out of Scalvaris?" he pried, fishing for weakness.

Omvar replied with silence. I gave him stone. I had to get through tonight, and then I'd be free and on my way home.

With my mate.

That was the truth I had to keep close to my heart.

The lamps guttered low. Skorai leaned close, his breath rank, voice oily. "Will your pet be sulking without you? Perhaps next season she can be our favored mascot. Can she fetch, or does she just bite?"

I met his eyes and counted three heartbeats before answering. "She bites on my command," I said, quiet enough that only he heard the edge beneath the words. Then I looked away, dismissing him.

Inside, my instincts screamed but I let no sign of

weakness show, no vulnerability. He was asking a lot about Vega—why? I scanned the room, guards, exits, distance to the nearest weapon. Still no chance to slip away. Skorai was ensuring his champions didn't vanish.

The party beat on. There was dancing. Revelry. Questionable closeness in the shadows on the outskirts of the hall. Finally, after some drunk slurred a tale of rebels impaled on the city walls, Skorai thumped the table. "Come now, champions. Rest peacefully tonight. Tomorrow, we spill your blood." His tone was all performance, his grin a locking manacle.

A cheer went up as he led us out of the hall.

We followed Skorai through narrow halls, the walls tight around us. Guards moved without speaking, their eyes sharp as vultures. Omvar's tread matched mine, both of us listening to each shift of stone, every rustle of Skorai's silks.

No path for escape.

Could I trust Omvar? Skorai seemed to resent him, and the man had shown kindness before. But finding me a healer and helping me free slaves were two different levels.

I couldn't risk it.

Up a twisting stair and down a corridor that

swallowed our footsteps. Skorai waved away the servants, his laugh trailing behind him like a stench. "Rest well. No assassins tonight. Not unless I send them." He laughed like it was a joke then gestured at the suite: silk-draped beds, gaudy lamps, bowls of overripe fruit.

Opulence that mocked. So like Ignarath.

Before Omvar could claim a space, Skorai pointed him to a bed near the fire. Control. The champion didn't flinch, just set himself down, his wings to the flames.

I stripped my leathers while Skorai lingered, his eyes digging into my spine. Washed my hands in a basin where the water smelled of metal. The lump in my throat was Vega's name. I forced it down. She would wait for me. She knew I was coming.

She just had to wait.

*Please,* veshari, *wait.*

Sleep came fitfully, always half aware of the guards outside, the weight of Skorai's laughter in the walls. It was a pretty cave. No one would leave it until dawn.

———

I rose before servants dared knock, my blood alive with old instinct. Breakfast arrived on heavy platters carried by downtrodden Drakarn servants, their claws filed down to nubs. Skorai's smug voice slithered in soon after. "The arena waits," he said. "Don't disappoint."

We stepped into a world alive with fevered cries. Drakarn hung from balconies, pressed against arches, their exclamations trailing us.

The arena loomed, a beast hungry to devour us all. Its stone jaws gaped wide, packed to bursting with a heedless, snarling horde. Banners whipped in the wind, red on black, Ignarath's colors cruel and unyielding. In the pit, the sand gleamed. Twelve guards stood there, shields ready, outlines sharp under the climbing sun.

What were they hiding? They formed a wall, shields held and wings flared slightly to block out whatever was behind them.

Something in my stomach curdled. I didn't like it.

They drove us to the edge. Skorai stalked forward, every movement a calculated flourish. The guards parted.

Silence. Heavy, unnatural.

And then I saw them.

Vega. Another human, the one called Kinsley. Huddled in the center, knees pressed to the stained sand. Their heads hung low beneath Ignarath's twin suns, glistening sweat and blood on their brows. Vega's hair clung to a gash on her temple, her jaw bruised purple. Kinsley swayed, barely clinging to consciousness, but still upright, still defiant.

The crowd roared. It surged, sensing the violence like a lava beast at the edge of a battle waiting to eat the dead.

Skorai lifted his hand, commanding the hush. "Today!" he roared. "The cycle ends in glory. But first, a gift for Ignarath!" His eyes cut into mine, then Omvar's, savoring the moment. "These outlanders are a stain on this land!"

The crowd got even wilder.

He turned toward us, eyes gleaming with the cruelty of an executioner. "Zarvash. Omvar. Execution is your privilege. Cleanse the sand, then meet as champions and settle this once and for all."

The arena boiled over, the masses shrieking for carnage. Thousands of fangs glittered in the morning light, their howls a single ravenous entity.

Heat pressed down, thick as chains. I measured distances, the guards, their spears, the weight of

Skorai's looming platform. Odds stacked high and merciless.

Omvar met my gaze. His expression revealed nothing, but his wings shifted. Was it some kind of sign? Omvar was the biggest unknown.

Would he help?

Vega lifted her head, her eyes finding mine. No fear there, only rebellion. Something twisted inside me, an old wound torn open again. I tasted iron.

Skorai believed he'd orchestrated our roles perfectly: execute, then duel.

One thing was certain: I would give him a show.

SKORAI WANTED A SHOW? Let him choke on it.

We were barely standing, both bruised and bleeding after a night in the worst kind of cell. Dead center in the arena's battered circle, surrounded by a dozen guards who looked eager to kill.

Each heartbeat felt like shards of glass grinding into bone. My shins throbbed as sand bit through torn trousers. The suns—because one wasn't enough on this hellhole—burned down, turning sweat into trails of humiliation.

Dragged here. Yanked like ragdolls. Dumped for the crowd to feast on. Dignity didn't make it through the gates. All I had left were lungs still sucking air and a pulse too stubborn to quit.

And Zarvash. He was looking at me like he'd

burn this place down the second he was given the chance.

We would do it together.

I didn't, for one second, let myself believe that this was the end.

The crowd's hunger crawled under the sand, clawing at my knees. Screeches, howls, each sound ricocheted off wood, ravenous. All for us. Fresh meat.

Kinsley knelt beside me, her breath rasping. A streak of dried blood and grit slashed her brow—a souvenir from our fight last night. Her jaw locked, eyes steady in that way people pretend they're fine. I saw the tremor beneath her skin.

Fear, maybe. Or just pure, grinding rage.

She watched me, as if to ask: *You said you trusted him. Was that a joke? Are we dead because of you?*

No time for words. They wouldn't save us anyway.

A guard strutted up, not the thug from before, but a blue-scaled brute with scarred jowls and predator eyes. He tossed two spears at our feet. *Spears* was generous. Sharp-ended stakes, crusted with old blood. Weapons that never got cleaned.

Survive if you can. Bleed if you can't.

Kinsley's voice came out dry as dust. "So this is it, huh?"

Nothing I could say wouldn't taste like ash. My world narrowed to tunnel vision, sharp and merciless. I grabbed a spear, hands numb from adrenaline. Kinsley took hers quietly, like a surgeon clutching a scalpel in a warzone. Her grip was awkward but firm. She didn't look at the weapon. She didn't have to. We both knew the odds.

Howls rose above us, a storm of scales, teeth, and sweat. The crowd's need pressed down like a fist on my neck.

*Block it out. Focus, Vega. Breathe.*

The ground scorched my knees. Every inhale scraped panic's edge, the air stinking of burnt copper and old blood from past executions.

Guards rattled their shields. Claws flexed, tails twitched. They were dying for an excuse.

And just past the guards was Zarvash. Hope twisted my gut, an ugly, dangerous spark.

Zarvash, taller than nightmares, bronze scales razor-sharp in the sun. Each step calculated, like he was two moves ahead of the violence. Omvar lumbered beside him, a wall of muscle and menace. Even standing still, he bent the air around him.

Omvar leaned in and muttered something. Zarvash flashed a grin that was all sharp teeth. Not comforting. More like a warning: whatever happens, it'll be real.

My heart stuttered. That cursed flicker of hope again.

We weren't dying today.

I hissed to Kinsley, voice shredded, "When they're close, hit the guard. Don't wait."

Kinsley's eyes went wide as saucers. She almost spat something, an insult, a curse, maybe just my name, but the chance slipped away. Zarvash and Omvar were already barreling forward, shoving through the ring. The crowd felt it too, a rising roar, the air thick with heat and sweat, each of us teetering on the edge of something violent.

I moved without thinking. No plan, no strategy. Just pure instinct, spear up, slamming the blunt end into a guard's wing. The shock rattled up my arm, but he staggered, just enough.

Then it all unraveled.

Chaos didn't just break loose, it detonated. Omvar bulldozed forward, ripping a spear from a guard's claws, snapping it across his knee and driving the jagged end home. Blood sprayed, hot and metallic. I felt it on my skin but didn't flinch.

Zarvash was a flicker of motion dipping under

blows, pivoting, striking fast. His foot came down on a guard's instep with a crunch that made my teeth clench. The guard barely had time to scream before Zarvash hauled him by his chains, swinging him into another like a wrecking ball.

Kinsley, trembling but furious, stayed low. She slashed her spear behind a scaly knee. Her opponent toppled, his claws grazing her hair as she jerked back. A tail whipped at her legs; she leapt over it, survival instincts stripping the fear from her eyes.

No time to think. Instinct ruled. I jabbed where armor parted, felt the sick give of scales and flesh, then the hot gush of viscous blood. My stomach lurched, but survival shoved the nausea aside. Hands slick on the shaft, grip slipping.

It didn't matter. Survive now, collapse later.

The guards regrouped, quick and brutal. Drakarn weren't for show; they were made for this. One swung a mace at Omvar, landing on his thigh. Omvar barely grunted, tore the weapon away, and brought it down on a head. The crunch rang out, a final deadly note.

Zarvash moved like a predator, spear spinning, blocking claws with the flat of his blade. He barked my name, sharp and urgent. I wanted to call back, but there were still too many guards. Kinsley ducked behind me, and we turned back-to-back, forming a circle of steel and defiance.

A spear sliced at my thigh, sharp, burning. Blood ran hot down my leg. I tore the weapon aside, slammed the butt into a guard's snout.

Crack.

Not enough. I hit him again, higher. His jaw clamped shut with a sick snap.

A shout, Zarvash's voice, or maybe my own, ripped through the din. A guard rammed me, shoulder to ribs, smashing me into Kinsley. Stars burst behind my eyes. Kinsley snarled, driving her spear under an exposed armpit. The wet, tearing sound turned my stomach.

This wasn't the battle I was made for. That was with blasters and guns, a bit of distance. Or a knife in the dark.

This? This was visceral.

The bodies piled up. Guards, snarling and battered, circled us. Three. Two. Then one, his eyes wild, tail lashing the sand, pure animal fear. Omvar lunged, his arm slick with blood, and twisted the helmet from the guard's head. A sickening snap. Silence.

I blinked, the world humming in my ears. Blood

dripped from my thigh, my legs trembling. Kinsley clutched her side, panting, eyes still fierce.

Zarvash loomed over me, breathing hard, his face streaked with blood and dust. One eye swollen nearly shut. He took in the carnage, then grabbed my shoulder.

His grip lit up fresh bruises down my arm. "Ready to get out of here?"

Omvar laughed, a deep, ragged sound that shook the air. It wasn't sane. It wasn't meant to be.

I tasted blood on my lip, grinned despite the pain. I wanted to kiss him. To hold him close and never let go. "We gave them the show. Let's leave before they send in reinforcements," I rasped.

Omvar laughed again, louder, throwing it at the crowd like a challenge. Above us, they teetered between horror and awe. The guards at the arena's edge froze, caught in their own shock. But not for long. They'd move; they always did. And the city would see us, Drakarn and humans, backs against the wall, fighting together.

Zarvash flared his wings and held out a hand. I didn't ask if they would hold. They had to. If not, we were dead.

Trust? I placed it all on Zarvash. No choice. Him or nothing.

Omvar was doing the same, waiting for Kinsley to join him. She glared for just a moment before her gaze darted to the crowd, and she picked her poison.

Omvar it was.

Zarvash wrapped his arms and tail around me and launched himself into the sky.

THE DAY BLED out over Ignarath's jagged skyline as we fled by ruined towers, shattered stone, every broken tooth of the city bathed in bruised purples and sickly gold. The air was thin, dry, laced with grit that scoured my scales. Freedom hung distant and uncertain.

The guards on the wall didn't shoot us down; they were looking for threats from the outlands, not fleeing champions. We made it past them before Skorai had a chance to warn them.

Flight was survival, nothing more. Below us, the desert sprawled in ripples of scarred earth and glassy sand, ancient lava flows coiling like dark veins. I didn't dare look back. I could feel Ignarath's menace trailing us, a tremor in the sky, a whisper of paranoia. The alarm hadn't rung yet, but that couldn't last.

Pain seared through me. Each stroke of my wings carved fresh agony into my shoulder. Weakness was a luxury I couldn't afford.

Vega clung to me, her arms locked, legs cinched tight. Her weight barely registered, but her tension did, sharp as a blade pressed to my side. She stared forward, unflinching, her mouth a hard line, her eyes fastened on the horizon. Not fear; she was made of something fiercer.

To my left, Omvar fought the air with brute strength. His wings battered the sky with heavy, forceful beats. He held Kinsley tight, his arm a steel band across her chest. Her hair whipped in the wind, her fist locked tight, knuckles white.

We skimmed low, hugging dead air. There was no pursuit yet, no horns, no shadows slicing across the stars. Ignarath's sentries were sluggish tonight, bloated on arrogance. A good night to gamble with fate. One misstep, and we'd be strung up for all to see.

Sweat burned my eyes. I angled us south, drawing on every scrap of knowledge I had of these lands, old patrol patterns, war plans that had never come to pass. My wounds screamed, trails of blood unraveling in the air behind me.

Minutes stretched, each one an eternity. The

city shrank. The desert yawned wide, its dunes pitted and scarred. When we reached the point where most escapees faltered, I banked sharply. Vega adapted instantly, her grip tightening, her eyes scanning for threats.

Darkness fell fully, thick and stifling. My muscles quaked, my wing close to giving out. When the next gust hit, a spear of pain drove into my shoulder. I couldn't push any farther.

"Landing," I growled. Vega said nothing, just braced for the descent.

Omvar circled, sweat glistening on his scales. I spotted a stretch of volcanic glass and twisted rock—no soft landings, but no cover for ambushes either. I angled down, coaxing the last ounce of strength from my battered wing. My feet hit hard. Pain exploded in my skull. I snarled, forced my legs to hold.

Vega slid off in silence, already scanning the shadows. Omvar crashed down beside me. Kinsley tumbled free, staggered, and dropped next to Vega, coughing on the dust.

Heat radiated off the stone, the night wind a thin, whining breath. Sweat traced lines over my scales. Blood, mostly mine, some from the guards, slicked my side. The air stank of scorched rock.

But we'd escaped. For now.

We crouched there, chests heaving, adrenaline fraying at the edges. Silence pressed in, sharp and heavy. Survival had its own bitter taste.

My wing throbbed, scales sticky with drying blood. Despite it all, I forced myself upright, scanning the horizon with clenched jaws, determined not to show how close I was to falling apart.

Vega was already scouring the perimeter, fingers tracing the earth like it might whisper secrets. She was all soldier now, compact, vigilant, no trace of softness. I watched her, a flicker of resentment flaring at how much I still hurt.

Fine.

"Set watch. No fire. We need to find supplies." My voice scraped like steel on stone. "There may be traders out here, or a village. We'll need water." The words were sharp, final.

Vega nodded, no argument. Kinsley dropped to her knees but forced herself up again, piecing herself together. Omvar, massive and unyielding, surveyed the dunes with a predator's patience. Out here, he seemed almost ... tamer. Or maybe just unshackled.

He spoke first. "Your wing's a wreck. You won't get far."

I bared my teeth. "I've flown on worse." A lie. "With luck, it'll mend before something comes to finish us." I threw the question back at him. "You could've stayed. Ignarath would've welcomed you. Drink, women, a fresh battle every night. Why throw that away?"

Omvar's face was stone. If the question cut, he swallowed it. Jaw tight, he stared into the night—dark as scorched ash. Then, his voice flat: "That life was rot. Glory?" he spat. "Just another fight. Another meal for the sand. Bleed for the crowd, die when they're bored. Your wings end up as someone's trophy."

His gaze flicked to me, eyes old and hollow. "I saw what the games did. Watched friends die for nothing, slaves butchered for lessons I stopped caring about. I felt nothing but disgust." He shrugged. "Then you showed up. Broke everything. Built something from the ruins. It made me remember I could still choose." His voice dropped. "I wanted to see if there was more."

I'd never heard him say so much. I wasn't sure if I trusted it. Ignarath wanted spies in Scalvaris. Helping me was a sure way in.

But I would be dead, *Vega* would be dead, if it weren't for him.

I coughed a dry laugh, hiding my fatigue. "You think Scalvaris will welcome you?"

Omvar's jaw clenched. "They might. I won't beg." Another shrug, heavy with weariness. "I have no home in Ignarath. Just ghosts. If there's a scrap of sanctuary on the other side, fine. If not, I'll wander." He meant it. Shoulders braced for exile.

Something in me wanted to spit. Old grudges. Old wounds.

I studied him, the way the shadows clung but never quite swallowed him. He wasn't an enemy. Not a friend, either. But he'd chosen, when the world had blades to our throats, he'd chosen us, knowing the cost. It was hard to hate that.

"They'll demand answers. Your blood, your secrets, every scar." My voice was gravel. "But I'll speak for you before the council." Saying it was a surprise even to me. "You have my word."

Omvar held my gaze, steady, bleak, accepting. "That'll do."

The night pressed in. Heat hung heavy, promising nothing but hunger and another grueling day.

No comfort. Not there.

Just survival. For tonight.

I wanted to take my mate and find a secluded spot, wanted to remind myself and her of what we were to one another. But there was no privacy there, no little cave or large boulder we could hide behind and lose ourselves in one another.

We had the darkness. And when she sat beside me, she took my hand in hers.

Comfort. At last.

BELOW US, Scalvaris sprawled like a beast guarding its hoard: arches jagged as broken ribs, keeps huddled tight, bridges thick as dragon spines. The wind carried the stench of the forges, molten metal, sulfur, the ghosts of old battles. I knew every scar in these caverns, every vow shattered there. The weight of it pressed into me, a brand of fear and home.

Inside, I was nerves and dread. We'd escaped Ignarath, but it was close, and we'd made enemies. The tensions between the two cities were already high. Had I started a war? Every wingbeat back felt like a gamble. The cost gnawed at me, each failure etched in Vega's bloodied face. My mate. My *veshari*. The one piece of myself I couldn't cover in armor.

She moved like she was unbreakable, blood

crusted on her jaw, that fire in her eyes. Fool. Warrior.

Mine.

At the thick doors of the Blade Council chambers, my claw struck true, the impact humming through me. Focus. Darrokar would have heard we were back. Scalvaris thrived on whispers—rumors slipping down tunnels, through markets, faster than blood.

I would have gone there first, but Kinsley and Omvar needed the attention of Mysha and her healers. And even if they were fine, the healing caverns were a safe place to stash them while I faced the wrath of Darrokar.

He wouldn't be happy about this.

The hall was thick with tension. Shadows clung to stone; voices died at our entrance. Drakarn, the Blade Council—watching. Vega's spine was a blade, and I forced myself to stand tall. Let them see control, not the exhaustion eating at me.

Darrokar crossed the hall in a flash, his black scales catching the light of the heat crystals embedded in the walls, anger coiled in every step. He stopped close—near enough to threaten, far enough to hold back. His eyes raked over me, assessing, then fixed on Vega. "So, you're alive. Both of you."

I swallowed the pain and spoke. "Ignarath is crawling with humans. A dozen, at least. Caged. Broken. Maybe five could fight. The rest are arena fodder. They've already sent others to the mines."

Vega's voice cut in, "Kira's sister is there. More humans from the same ship we were on. They're being tortured, enslaved. Some are already dead."

"And how did you find all this out?" He sounded ready to make someone bleed. Me? Ignarath? I couldn't know.

I gave him the whole story, even the parts that made me look like a weak fool. Our capture, my injury. Fighting in the arena and fleeing before the winner could be chosen.

Some would call me a coward for that last part. Especially when I told them of Omvar.

The council shifted, murmurs rustling. Darrokar's gaze didn't waver. "You expect me to shelter an Ignarath dog?"

I clenched my jaw. "He saved my mate. Pulled her from Skorai's claws." I let the word hang: *mate*. It was a declaration, a blade with no sheath.

The hall went still. Eyes pinned me. I held them all, dared them to challenge.

Beside me, Vega sucked in a harsh breath and cut me an even harder look. It occurred to me that I should have made a declaration to her before I made it before the council. But instead of rejecting it, she took a step closer and let her arm brush mine.

Perhaps some things could be unsaid and still count.

Darrokar's expression flickered with something sharp, almost respect. "That is unexpected." Not a question. "Especially from you." His gaze shifted to Vega. "And you. Do you accept this bond, Vega Cross?"

Vega shot me a look. Then she grinned. "Someone has to put up with him. It may as well be me."

There was a choked laugh from somewhere in the council. Possibly Vyne, if I recognized the edge in his voice. I didn't dare turn away from Darrokar. There was no love lost between us, and he held my fate in my hands. Nothing Vega and I had done in Ignarath was sanctioned. He could exile me, execute me, strip me of my council position for insubordination.

I had friends on the council, or I *had* before Vega. None of them would accept our bond.

So I would make new friends. New allies. Build

myself up once more. As long as I had her, nothing mattered.

Darrokar let the silence stretch. "Sanctuary isn't yours to offer. The council will decide his place. Until then, Omvar is your burden. If he betrays us, you kill him before anyone else suffers."

I nodded, my voice hard. "Agreed."

He scanned us both, his eyes a blade. "You've seen the filth that covers Ignarath. Was it worth it?"

Vega stepped forward, her voice unyielding. "We can't abandon the humans there. There are fighters. Healers. Kira's *sister*. They don't deserve their fate."

Darrokar's jaw tightened. "It's not just about deserving. Ignarath is strong. If we steal the humans, we court war."

Vega's fingers brushed my arm. "Some wars are worth fighting," she said.

The council pressed in, scales glistening under heat crystals, suspicion thick as smoke. Warriors crowded the hall—Vyne, Rath, Khorlar—while whispers coiled like snakes. Darrokar's mate, Terra, lingered in the shadows, her gaze pinned on Vega.

He thought about it for several beats. "The council will consider this. Ignarath will not toy with us."

My mate's shoulders sagged, and I wrapped my wing around her, pulling her close.

Darrokar spun away, barking orders; messengers, aides, council members scattered under his command. The hall erupted with voices crackling with fear and hope, rumors spilling like wildfire.

In the chaos, I caught Vega's hand, scarred and strong, fitting mine perfectly. She held on, no resistance, just a fierce, silent bond.

We slipped into the corridors, walls heavy with secrets. My mind churned, losses mounting, rage smoldering, her scent fanning every risk I'd taken. My career, my standing, my life, all of it was at risk now. The Forge Temple would hear about this soon. Karyseth would be barging in, demanding answers and sacrifices. Mektar would call me a traitor.

But Vega was at my side.

A final door shut behind us, council noise snuffed out in an instant. Just us. No masks. Nowhere to hide.

I turned to her, voice stripped bare. "Come back with me. To my quarters."

Her grin was crooked, weary, a cut on her lip splitting faintly. "As long as you keep the chains to yourself this time."

Laughter broke free, easing the ache for a moment. "Never again," I vowed.

We moved through the caverns, the light from heat crystals dancing over bruises, sentries' eyes like daggers. I kept her close. The city watched. Let it. I'd gut anyone who dared threaten her now. My oath wasn't to Scalvaris anymore, not truly.

It was to her, and gods help me, I'd bleed to make it count.

I WAS WALKING with Zarvash through the walls of Scalvaris. It would have been shocking if I didn't want him so much.

This wasn't a gentle hunger. It was sharp, edged with fear and desire. Every brush of his claws against my skin sent a jolt through me, my body alive with wanting.

If desire was a language, my body was speaking directly to him.

He led me around a final corner, and there it was: a massive door, carved and bound with iron, sigils from the Forge Temple etched deep in its surface. Zarvash pressed his palm against a glyph, and the door opened with a low groan. Once we stepped inside, he sealed it shut.

We were alone.

Finally.

The air was hot, heavy. Heat crystals cast shadows that danced along the walls. The room was stark, honest: a battered platform for a bed, weapons mounted above, blades and spears that spoke of countless battles. Silks and furs lay tangled on the floor, a riot of color against stone. It smelled of him, of sweat and steel and something darker.

He stood by the door, chest heaving, claws flexing as if he were holding himself back. This wasn't Zarvash, the reserved council member of Scalvaris. This was the beast inside him, barely contained. His eyes locked on mine, and I felt stripped bare. He didn't see me as a threat, a weapon.

He saw me as his.

Thank fucking god.

Then he moved, crossing the space between us in a heartbeat. His hand shook slightly as he pushed my hair back, the tip of a claw grazing my cheek. Goosebumps spread across my skin.

"Vega," he said, my name rough in his throat. It sounded like a vow. And then he kissed me.

There was no hesitation. His mouth crashed against mine, his tongue demanding, unyielding. I tasted iron, felt the sharp edge of a fang against my lip. I gasped, and he swallowed the sound, pulling me closer. My body arched against him, desperate for more. His hand tangled in my hair, tilting my head so he could take even deeper.

When he finally pulled back, we were both panting. His eyes burned into mine, and a single word slipped from his lips: *"Veshari."*

It wasn't a question. It was a declaration, everything unsaid between us in that one word.

His hands found the hem of my tunic. "Let me," he murmured, his voice careful, almost trembling. I nodded, lifting my arms. This wasn't surrender. It was need, transformed into something else entirely.

Fabric parted.

Collarbone, then shoulder, then breast. His thumb brushed old scars, claws traced the shrapnel trail along my ribs. Each new patch of skin catalogued, not devoured. Reverence, not pity. He bent, pressed his mouth to scar tissue. My bullet wound. The old burn. Each one a benediction in Drakarn, words I only half understood, but felt shiver-flush between us, deeper than fluency.

His tongue traced a scar just below my breast. I bit back a moan. Shame vanished, leaving only the heat skittering down my spine, nipples peaked to harsh points, his breath a meteor trail in the warm air.

This close, his scales pressed to my skin, heat rolled off bronze and copper as my fingers clawed at his clothes, clumsy with need. He caught my hands, stilled me with a laugh that fractured at the edges.

"Too slow," he growled. The fabric ripped aside, discarded. His chest a battlefield map, muscle knotted over old wounds; fresh ridges erupting along his shoulder. I touched the biggest scar, a crescent, old, ragged.

He caught my hand, kissed the knuckle.

His wings trembled. Too close, veins showing, old scars black under crystal light. I ran my hands over his chest, doing my own star mapping. His gasp tightened my belly. I wanted to taste every wound, wanted to catalog him, memorize him, archive him into muscle memory.

He bent to suck my nipple into his mouth. Teeth grazed, tongue circled, heat spiked—each rotation ratcheted tension higher. I writhed, back arching, thighs squirming, skin rubbing hot against scale.

"More," I gasped. Need, unfiltered.

He answered with teeth, deeper suction, tongue flicking sharp. Swollen skin desperate when he moved on.

His tail—devilish rope that it was—slithered between my thighs, circling, anchoring, tip pulsing like a second heart. He pressed me against his hips, I felt his cock, thick and burning, gouging my belly, smearing wetness across the bare skin there. I gasped, obscene, involuntary. My core ached.

I needed him.

Zarvash lifted me, effortless, arms under my thighs, hauling me up like I weighed nothing. Not gentle, not cruel, just hunger incarnate. He carried me to the platform, laid me among silk, my skin prickling, fever-bright, nerves sparking. He knelt between my knees, wings mantled, intensity frightening. Focused. Worshipful. Possessive.

His bed was an altar, and I was his sacrifice.

He spread my thighs wide.

"You're drenched." His voice was gone to gravel. His hands shook as blunt claws dug into my hips.

His tongue was perfect. Alien. Too long, too hot, ridged and sensate. He licked me slow, a surveyor testing new ground as if this was the first time. My hips jerked, vision going fuzzy. He lapped, pausing only to groan. The sound vibrated in my bones. He sucked and sucked, mouth greedy, chin wet with me.

My hands fisted in his hair. My hips rolled up, desperate. "Za—fuck—Zarvash!"

He hummed against me. Vibration climbed my spine—a tuning fork, set to my pleasure. His tongue traced me, dove shallow, then deep. Flick, flick, wriggle—no human mouth remotely this precise. Each lap stole breath and logic. The ridges tormented, every drag of rough velvet, and somewhere deep: a spark that leapt the gap, half physical, half chemical. Our bond, alive and burning.

He fixed his mouth over my core. Suction, then a flurry of flicks, slow circles with the flat. I pleaded, high-pitched, almost a laugh: "Please, please, don't stop—" My thighs shook. I was clawing at his skull. The orgasm came, sudden as a solar flare, convulsing everything.

I screamed, a sound ricocheting through the stone.

He kept drinking, didn't let go, a hunter at the well. When I shuddered, twitching, he pressed his face to my thigh, inhaled like he'd found a rare mineral vein. His eyes fluttered, drag-addled.

He traced me with his tongue, scraping up every drip. "You taste like fire." Voice starved. "Like mine."

His tail found my entrance and slipped in, stretching, thick, perfect. I keened, helpless. There was a burn, strange and delicious, almost electric.

"*Veshari.*" He was pleading now, as if I could say no. "Your scent, your taste—it's everywhere, inside me, in my blood."

He drew up, chest heaving, lips glossed with me. "You need to see what's yours."

He knelt upright, wings wide. Body on open display: scales black-to-red studded at his hips, that ridge at his cock's base. The shaft: thick, nothing human—veins swelling like fault lines, the red flesh coated in sweat and more. Foreskin—its alien shape, not just a layer but a living, flexible lip capping the crown, twitching, eager, twitching at the air. I saw the glistening notch, the tongue, lapping for scent, almost sentient, the want built into biology. Pre-cum shimmered at the tip, viscous, musky, impossible. I inhaled smoke, salt, the blueprint of desire.

My hand lifted. I traced from scale-knotted base over the fever-hot shaft, feeling heat and heart and want. The cock-lip nuzzled my palm, sucking, writhing, hungry. I circled his cock with both hands; the lip clung, tongue seeking. I pressed my thumb into the slit—the tongue curled to meet me. Zarvash grabbed my wrist, bracing, not stopping.

His body rocked into my grip. "*Veshari—*" His voice was a wrecked thing. "If you ... keep ..."

I bent to taste him. The head was velvet and hot, flavor star sharp, all smoke and salt. The lip at its tip flicked into my mouth—tongue, seeking. I let it. Zarvash's tail thudded, wings snapped.

Fluid slid over my tongue, briny, alive; I could almost taste the mating bond in my blood.

"Enough." Zarvash's growl shook with effort and want. Command and plea, indivisible. "If you keep —" His desperation bled through. "Let me. Let me claim—"

I slid back on trembling limbs. "Please." Strange, how thin my voice was. How full of want.

He hovered over me. Cock flushed, dripping— the scent marked me already, musk and fire and a touch of ozone. He guided himself to my entrance, patient through agony. "Slowly," he gritted, every word a brand new fracture of will.

I hooked my legs high, opening, inviting. The head pressed my slit, tongue whorled over my clit, gathering slick. I gasped, bucked. He dragged the crown lower, circling, until at last it pressed into my entrance.

I exhaled and bore down and invited him deeper. He groaned, sank in, a slow, torturous thrust, the fullness exquisite. When his hips were flush, I felt the scales of his base pressure my clit, the cock's tongue twining inside me, that living lip teasing, tugging, coating me in him.

Marked. Occupied. Claimed.

He bowed his forehead to mine. "Mine. My mate. No one—" His voice failed, choked by feeling.

I found his wings, membranes trembling. I stroked along the veins; he shuddered, cock twitching. He caught my wrists, pinned them overhead, caging me open. His hips rocked slow, each stroke a seismic fault, vein after vein massaging my nerves, the cock's tongue licking at my g-spot, a star's pulse in the dark. My sex squeezed, milking; my body painted in slick and musk and wanting.

His rhythm shredded. Tail lashed, curled tight around my hips, yanking me into every thrust. Jaw snapped. Drakarn curses spilled loose, words older than fire.

Instinct drove me, and I bit him on the shoulder, hard, nails raking his scales, leaving my own constellation of marks.

Fang grazed my neck, not to break, but to promise. Dangerous, but the threat only carved safety deeper.

Friction built. Each slap of skin catalyzed a new chemical reaction inside me, heat, tension, ache. The pressure inside wound tighter, his cock stretching, tongue working, tail holding, wrists bound, mind fracturing.

Release tore through me, no warning, only

rupture. I convulsed, gripping his cock, milking. Zarvash threw his head back, howled, animal, ancient, shattered, hips driving, cock swelling, then the rush: his flood inside, thick, musky.

I shivered, starlight under skin, nerves jangled, skin streaked with sweat, and the undeniable evidence of us.

Zarvash fell atop me, weight caging me in, tail, arms, even wings enclosing. Still inside me, body still pulsing, leaking, his want embedded everywhere.

Our sweat merged, our scent blurred. His tongue slicked over my jaw, throat, ear, lapping up the mess, the salt of tears I didn't remember crying. Each kiss a promise. Possession and worship, not mutually exclusive after all.

He murmured between kisses, words, rough as gravel, nearly broken: "Mine. You wear my scent. None will hurt you. You are home."

My hands traced his spine, found the ridged valley there. I stroked; he twitched, bucked, nearly sobbed. "You're trembling," I whispered, voice barely there. "Did I—"

He bundled himself around me, all tail, all muscle, all wing. His scales slicked up my thighs; our combined fluids still sticky-hot between. His tongue searched the bite mark at my shoulder, slow, careful, cleaning, soothing. Drawing out the hurt, making it a memory.

"Everyone will know," he whispered, breath tangled in my hair, all possessive satisfaction. "No one can challenge what's carried in your scent. You're mate-claimed."

I inhaled deep. My skin reeked of him, inside, outside, every gland rewritten, my own musk altered, burned new into memory. Pheromones as proof, as claim, as inheritance.

Hushed, only the rasp of breath, the quake of spent adrenaline, the biological signature of what we'd done. Then—

"Did you ever imagine," Zarvash asked, voice full of things I couldn't read, "that it would ever end this way?"

I ghosted my mouth to his jaw, eyes closed against the hazardous hope. "Not in a million years."

He tucked his chin over my crown, tension leaking out, weight flooding into the shelter of his body. Drakarn devotion, cocooned and complete. For the first time since falling to this violent world, my chest unclenched. I exhaled into the heat of belonging.

LAST NIGHT HAD LEFT its mark—literal marks, fresh on my neck. I wore them like a badge of honor. Every swallow reminded me they were there. And the ache between my legs? It was well earned.

Zarvash's scent haunted me, clinging stubbornly to my hair, beneath my skin. There would be no doubt who I belonged to. Who belonged to me.

But the city had its own demands, louder and fiercer than my own. So, I shoved it all down and headed for the human quarters.

I found Kinsley sprawled on the floor outside my room, legs splayed, head tipped back as she breathed in shallow gulps of thick air. She clocked me, her hand darting to the knife at her side, a quick warning in her eyes. She never let her guard down. I respected that.

Reika crouched nearby, jabbing frustrated fingers at a battered comm device that had been scavenged from our downed ship. I knew Orla liked working on broken tech; maybe Reika was learning from her. Reika's hair was a wild mess, her eyes sunk deep in a face stretched thin by anxiety with nowhere to go. Kinsley watched her like a hawk, tension stringing the air tight between them.

"When were you planning to tell me that the lizard was more than your partner?" Kinsley demanded.

Reika glared and turned away from me while the others—Selene, Orla, Kaiya—turned my way, eyes wide. It was a party.

Wonderful.

"If I told you, would you have risked escaping?" If I was in her shoes, my answer would be a hearty hell no. Even with the taste of Zarvash embedded deep in me, I still have a default level distrust of this place that told me to be on my guard.

Kinsley shot me a sideways glance, suspicion still lurking in her eyes. "I had a right to know."

Maybe she did. It didn't make me regret my decision.

Eden's shoes squeaked on the stone. She was too bright, too young for this place, but she had a knack for fitting in. She swiped a smudge off her cheek with her thumb. Her hands wouldn't quite stay still. She was young, only twenty, though her eyes said otherwise, sharp, jumpy, always scanning the room for something.

"How did Kira take the news?" I kept my voice low, not wanting to stir the tension. I should have told her myself, but I'd been a bit ... distracted.

Eden's gaze darted away. "Not good." She pressed her lips together, her pulse flickering fast in her throat. "She's locked herself in her room. Won't let anyone in. I left her some food. She'll come out when she's ready." She tried to sound casual, but I heard the worry beneath it.

Guilt twisted inside me. I'd promised Kira answers, a rescue. Instead, I'd handed her fresh grief. Classic me—kick down a door, forget about the collateral damage.

Before the silence could thicken, Terra stormed in, ponytail swinging, boots kicking up dust. Her eyes found me immediately, electric and wild. She didn't bother with a greeting.

"Are you fucking kidding me?" she demanded, her voice crackling with barely contained energy.

I arched a brow. "You'll have to be more specific, Captain."

There was really only one thing she could be talking about, and she'd been there for the declaration. This wasn't about confirmation; it was to make me eat crow.

To say I'd hated the Drakarn over these last few months was an understatement. That I was now snuggled up next to one who'd nearly gotten Orla killed? Yeah, this was going to take some getting used to.

She stepped closer, arms folded tight. "You and Zarvash?"

I met her stare, unflinching. "Yes."

Her jaw dropped. Delight sparked in her eyes, feral and shameless. "Ha!"

Behind her, Selene let out a snort, and Kaiya's lips curved into an uncontrollable grin.

Terra gasped, dripping with mock outrage. "Vega Cross—Miss I Hate the Drakarn—hooked up with a seven-foot lizard tactician. If you'd bet me—" She pointed at me, her voice dropping to a conspiratorial whisper. "You're sure he's not got you under mind control? Alien pheromones?" Her eyes sparkled with mischief.

Eden wheezed while Kaiya's grin bordered on wicked.

I leveled a glare at them. "One: If there is alien

mind control, it's not like I'm the only one. Two: talk to the doc about alien pheromones. Three: Anyone who says 'Vega's gone soft' will learn what a melted face feels like."

Someone giggled. A real, honest giggle; my dignity never stood a chance.

Terra eyed me like I was a ticking bomb. "You nearly slit Darrokar's throat just for talking that first week. I thought you would never speak to me again after we got together. What changed? Tell me it was the tail."

I groaned, burying my face in my hands. "No details, you vultures. Also—" My voice caught, just for a second. "Nope, never mind. You don't deserve it."

Terra, relentless, leaned in. "It's the whole thing, huh? The full claiming, scent marking, mated thing?"

I shot her a glare that could kill. "Let's just say I'm sleeping well. That enough for you? Go ask Hawk about her love life if you need more. Or do you want us asking about you and Darrokar?"

Silence. Terra had a stare that could peel paint.

Eden, bless her, clapped her hands once and broke it: "Who's spreading the word? Is this a city-wide holiday? Should I sneak out for more wine?"

I snorted. "If Scalvaris partied every time a human hooked a Drakarn, they'd burn through their rations by sunrise."

Something in my chest loosened. The air felt lighter, the danger a distant hum. "For the record, I'm still emotionally stunted, extremely suspicious, and allergic to group therapy. This just ... happened."

Terra laughed. "Drinks all around. Also, I need the details; Orla's running a betting pool."

I scowled. "You had a pool?"

She smirked. "Obviously. Odds were four-to-one you'd stab a Drakarn before you'd sleep with one. Some of us got creative. Hawk owes me big."

"Perfect. Did anyone bet on bronze scales in particular?"

Terra shook her head. "No one was that stupid."

Something knotted in my chest went loose. Just a little. Enough to breathe.

"I'll try not to let it tank my reputation," I said, my voice close to breaking.

Terra's grin was wide and sharp. "Too late, Cross. Welcome to the lizard-wranglers' club."

Laughter smudged the tension, turning it into something warm. Eden leaned in, conspiratorial: "So

... is his tail as impressive up close as it looks from here? And does it really—?"

"Say one more word, and I will show you that I can still use a knife."

Eden just laughed.

## ZARVASH

They watched us.

Drakarn eyes, calculating, their nostrils flaring as we passed. Some bared teeth; others looked away, hiding curiosity under a veil of unease. I heard the whispers: *Zarvash claimed a human.*

The Forge Temple acolytes turned their yellow robed backs on us as we passed. Karyseth had already cursed me. But Jalliun, another priest, had invited me to dine at his table. The temple wasn't all fanatics. And not all eyes glared.

When she walked beside me, chin high, shoulders square, worries shrank to nothing.

Our quarters were a fortress against the world. Four stone walls, a heavy door, privacy that was only ours. All that mattered. She moved through the dim light, braid loosening, bruises fading across her jaw. Tired, but unyielding. I watched her, needing the strength she gave me.

Habit took over: strip out of my leathers, assess my still healing wing, gulp water in silence. The flight from Ignarath had done me no favors, and Mysha had yelled at me for more than an hour when I finally went to see her. Vega sat on the edge of the sleeping platform, flicking grit from her sleeves. Light from the crystals painted her skin in gold and red, tracing every bruise. I counted her injuries. I kept score.

One day, Ignarath would pay for every drop of her blood a hundredfold.

"Sit," she said, voice rough but steady. I obeyed.

My wing throbbed with each heartbeat. She unwound the bandages carefully, her hands stable no matter how I flinched. Over the last week, this had become our ritual.

She shoved a mug of water filled with herbs into my hands. "Drink. Collapse on me, and I'll leave you where you lie."

I smirked. "It takes more than this to finish me." But I tossed back the drink with a grimace. The healing herbs were bitter and made my wing burn even more.

But there was something more than pain, something that had been on my mind since my discussion with Jalliun.

"I want our bond recognized at the Forge Temple."

I felt her breath hitch, watched her brace as if I'd struck her. Her voice was pure disbelief. "You're insane. Orla and Rath barely survived the Temple's games. You want to offer them our throats?"

I wanted to reach out and hold her, to cradle her close, but I knew she needed the space to think. "No trial. No spectacle. Just vows. Public, open. I want all of Scalvaris to know you're mine."

She blinked. Something flickered in her eyes. She fought it, swiping at her eyes before looking at me with an expression she would give no one else. "Zarvash, this is so new. We're just—"

I took her hands in mine. No retreat. "You're my mate. There is nothing new about it. This is an ancient thing. A timeless thing. You and I. Always. I would have died in Ignarath, in more ways than one without you. I want witnesses. I want every scale in this city to see it."

Silence still. Then her mouth twitched. "You want them to know you lost a bet to a human?"

I growled. "Be serious. I chose. Fate chose. Anyone who doesn't like it can choke."

She squeezed my hand, rough as ever, then pulled my face down for a kiss. Not soft. Fierce, like we might devour each other before the city could. Salt, ash, sweat, and need. I drank her in, jaw aching, fists closing around air. Should've stopped. Didn't. This, here, was the only thing that fit.

We pulled apart, breath ragged. Her forehead rested against mine.

She stared, a crooked smile bending her lips. "You think this is easy? You want a Temple oath? We'll be lucky if Karyseth doesn't burn us."

I bared my teeth, grinning. "I didn't limp out of Ignarath for easy."

She laughed, sharp and defiant. The world outside bristled with rumors and steel. None of it mattered. Not here.

She caught the spikes of my jaw and pulled me closer. "Fine. Your way. Let them try."

The satisfaction was almost mean. Not hope. That was dangerous.

I pressed my lips to her brow, soft, just long

enough to remember it. "I'll arrange it," I said. "Let them come."

She kissed me again, all teeth and need. I let her take everything she wanted, answered with something just as rough.

I prowled the city's paths, wings tucked tight, senses razor-sharp. Suspicion clung to me. Every glance was a dagger, expecting violence, despising my presence. This place was nothing like Ignarath, but there were echoes in the distrust. They call me *friend*, but I hear the hiss behind it. Outlander. Unworthy. I'd never be one of them.

But I wasn't there for their trust.

I'd lied when I told Zarvash why I was helping him.

I was on the hunt.

The river carved through the city, cold and relentless. Its chill soaked into the black stone despite the natural heat of the caves. Scalvaris hunched over that current: bridges, ramparts, walls pressed tight to squeeze out anything that didn't belong. Anything like me.

Younglings cackled where the water fanned out, their scales soft, wings flapping. They were unscarred, foolish enough to think play kept the monsters away. I watched from the shadows. My tail twitched.

One child stilled, bright green eyes locking on me. He ducked behind a bigger girl—red-scaled, sharp-chinned. Smart. Survival meant knowing where and when to hide.

A cold draft stirred the river, its glow shifting like fireflies. Brief, savage beauty. I could almost be seduced into staying there all day.

Her scent found me first—sweet, alien, cut with copper and fear. Human. Not just any.

*Her.*

I'd trailed echoes of her through twisting alleys, always a step behind. More than once, I thought I found her only to turn up empty. But that scent anchored me. Warm skin, sweet, impossible softness.

My fangs itched. Hunger, hot and unwelcome.

Then I saw her. Across the bank, haloed in the river's glow. Small, vulnerable, but her stance was tight. Hair shorn short, arms moving with careful deliberation. A human at ease is a lie.

This one never stopped watching for trouble.

I drank her in. A mistake. Every line, her shadow, the tension under her skin, set my scales twitching. I remembered her scent on desert wind, remembered sand baking it into my bones. I'd chased that trail, let hope and fury tangle me.

Now, seeing her alive, the old need flared.

She crouched at the water's edge, hands busy with a woven satchel, sunlight catching on her arm. She moved like someone who expected the world to collapse. Every motion carved by hardship. I tasted guilt and hunger, burning together.

And then another voice cut through.

"Reika, let's go."

Another human: taller, golden-skinned, jagged with vigilance. I didn't know her name. Eyes sweeping, never lingering.

Reika's head snapped up, and she saw me. Her eyes widened a fraction before she turned towards the other human and nodded, saying something I couldn't hear.

The taller woman murmured, "Come on, we have to go."

They moved past the Drakarn children, who splashed aside. Reika glanced back, only for a second, and not looking at me then let herself be drawn to where more humans huddled under a carved arch. The city closed around them.

I stayed, claws curling until pain replaced need. I'd crossed half a continent, risked everything, trailing her scent like a curse. And I got only her back, her silence.

But the hunt wasn't over.

She was alive. That knowledge settled, a dark comfort, hissing under my skin, fueling the ache that never quite settled.

She was alive.

And for now, that had to be enough.

## NEED A LITTLE MORE OF ZARVASH & VEGA?

Sign up at the link below to **receive a free bonus epilogue!**

**Get your free bonus epilogue!**

https://katerudolph.net/index.php/zarvash-bonus/

———

# Thank you so much for reading *Chained to the Champion*!

Your support means the world to me. If you enjoyed the story, it would mean even more if you could take a moment to share your thoughts in a review or leave a rating.

Hearing from readers like you makes all the difference!

———

*What's next in this series:*

### *Beast of Ash and Blood*

**Drakarn Mates**

A HARSH DESERT PLANET. Stranded humans. Draconic aliens. A match made in... well, somewhere.

*Claimed by the Drakarn Warrior Lord*
*Echoes of Fire*
*Scorched by Fate*
*Fated to the Drakarn Commander*
*Chained to the Champion*
*Beast of Ash and Blood*

———

**Dragon Brides**

## Dragon Princes. Fierce Women. Love.

Fated mates, fierce women, and dragon princes are
ready to find their mates.

### *Also available in audio!*

*Crux*

*Ranger*

*Saber*

*Cipher*

*Storm*

*Drake*

*Asher*

*Knox*

*Flint*

*Pine*

———

## Guarded by the Shifter

## Werewolf. Bodyguard. Mate.

The origins of these shifters are shrouded in mystery,
but they're determined to protect their mates from
any harm that comes their way.

### *Also available in audio!*

*Hunting Season*

*On the Prowl*

*Stalking Magic*
*Hungry for the Wolf*
*Wolf Cursed* (novella)
*Wolf's Temptation*

———

**Stealing the Alpha**

**The thief takes what she wants, but the alpha keeps what's his...**
Join shifter thief Mel as she clashes with lion alpha Luke in an explosive trilogy of two opposites who can't keep away from one another.
***Also available in audio!***
*The Alpha Heist*
*Entangled with the Thief*
*In the Alpha's Bed*

———

**Alien Mates: Planet Exile**

Guerran is no place for pretty human women. But these alien heroes will protect their mates!
**Also available in audio!**

Exile's Hunter
Exile's Adored

———

## Zulir Warrior Mates

### Kidnapped humans. Alien Warriors. Electric wings.

The Zulir Warrior Mates series brings you human heroines and heroes abducted from Earth who find love – and wings! – with the alien warriors who rescue them.

***Also available in audio!***

*Synnr's Saint*
*Synnr's Hope*
*Synnr's Spark*
*Synnr's Kiss*
*Synnr's Ride*

———

## Mated to the Alien

### Fated Mate Alien Romance

Detyens are doomed to die young if they don't find

their fated mates.

Follow along as these mated pairs fight off aliens, corrupt dictators, prejudiced humans, pirates, and more! The books can be read or listened to in any order, though some characters show up in multiple stories.

***Select books available in audio.***

Pick a book and jump into the action today!

*Ruwen*

*Tyral*

*Stoan*

*Cyborg*

*Krayter*

*Kayleb*

*Shayn*

*Braxtyn*

*Doryan*

*Dekon*

———

**Detyen Warriors**

**Detya was destroyed a hundred years ago. These doomed warriors are out to find justice... and their mates.**

The Detyen Warriors series brings you kick butt heroines, alpha alien heroes, fated mates, and relationships strong enough to span the galaxy!

**The entire series is also available in audio!**

*Soulless*

*Ruthless*

*Heartless*

*Faultless*

*Endless*

———

**Detyen Warrior Outcasts**
**Fated Mate Alien Romance**

These doomed warriors were abandoned by their people and live on the edge. Their mates hold the key to their salvation.

Pick a book and jump into the action today!

***Also available in audio!***

*Dangerous Bond*

*Intrepid Bond*

*Wayward Bond*

———

## Alien Holiday Romance

Christmas... in space????
These alien holiday romances look beyond Earth's winter holidays and ring in the season across the galaxy!

***Select titles available in audio***.

*Snowed in with the Alien Beast*
*The Alien's Winter Gift*
*The Alien Reindeer's Wild Ride*
*Trapped with her Alien Mate*

————

## Alien Outlaws

**Outlaws, schemes, and love... it's all there in the Alien Outlaws series...**

Andie Munster is sick of life on Ixilta, the planet she got dumped on after being abducted from Earth six years ago. And when the mysterious and dangerous Xandr shows up looking for a way off the planet, she's half-prisoner, half-co-conspirator in a wild rush to escape.

***Also available in audio!***

*Rogue Alien's Escape*

*Rogue Alien's Woman*
*Rogue Alien's Secret*
*Rogue Alien's Legacy*

———

**Find more by Kate Rudolph at** www. katerudolph.net

# ABOUT KATE RUDOLPH

KATE RUDOLPH IS a paranormal and sci-fi romance writer who lives in Indiana. She loves writing about kick butt heroines and the steamy heroes who love them. She's been devouring romance novels since she was too young to be reading them and had to hide her books so no one would take them away. She couldn't imagine a better job in this world than writing romances and sharing them with her fellow readers.

If you enjoyed this story, please consider leaving a review.

www.ingramcontent.com/pod-product-compliance
Lightning Source LLC
Chambersburg PA
CBHW061638190726
48289CB00006B/1648